W9-BNU-334

"Dance with me."

Rhiannon smiled her agreement to Shawn's request. He pulled her to her feet and onto the intimate dance floor. And as his arms closed around her, he inhaled as though breathing her in.

The song was a whisper and a plea. A promise made.

His right hand was on her waist, his fingers resting against the curve of her side while his left hand cradled her right. Heat emanated from him, working its way through her until he was all she could feel. In those long, intimate moments in his arms, all she knew was him.

She simply relaxed and enjoyed the sensations coursing through her. She remembered for a moment what it was like to be seventeen and feeling the sweet ache of desire for the very first time.

She never wanted the music to end.

Dear Reader,

I'm very excited to bring you Rhiannon's story, a follow-up to my July 2010 Harlequin Superromance novel, *Beginning with Their Baby.* From the moment Rhiannon appeared, I knew I wanted to tell her story, and I'm so blessed to have an editor who told me to "go for it." Writing this novel was bittersweet, as one of its themes—a woman recovering from violence—is a subject near and dear to my heart. When I was in college, I volunteered at a woman's shelter and was absolutely horrified and astounded at what so many of the women had gone through to arrive there. Watching them heal was an incredible thing, and their bravery made an impact on me that has lasted ever since.

In this novel my heroine, Rhiannon, is recovering from a brutal rape that cost her her career, her marriage and her sense of self. She's spent the past few years healing slowly, but it is not until she is confronted with Shawn—a handsome, talented, easygoing younger man—that she really begins to see herself as a healthy, strong woman again. The relationship between Shawn and Rhiannon was difficult to write, as it is complex and full of emotional ups and downs, but getting them (two people who so richly deserve it) to their happy ending was a thrill for me. I hope you enjoy reading *Unguarded* as much as I enjoyed writing it.

I love to hear from my readers—either by email at tracy@tracywolff.com or on my blog, tracywolff.blogspot.com. Stop by and say hello sometime.

All my best,

Tracy Wolff

Unguarded
Tracy Wolff

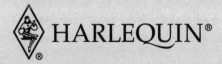

HARLEQUIN®

TORONTO • NEW YORK • LONDON
AMSTERDAM • PARIS • SYDNEY • HAMBURG
STOCKHOLM • ATHENS • TOKYO • MILAN • MADRID
PRAGUE • WARSAW • BUDAPEST • AUCKLAND

If you purchased this book without a cover you should be aware
that this book is stolen property. It was reported as "unsold and
destroyed" to the publisher, and neither the author nor the
publisher has received any payment for this "stripped book."

Recycling programs
for this product may
not exist in your area.

ISBN-13: 978-0-373-71676-0

UNGUARDED

Copyright © 2010 by Tracy L. Deebs-Elkenaney

All rights reserved. Except for use in any review, the reproduction or
utilization of this work in whole or in part in any form by any electronic,
mechanical or other means, now known or hereafter invented, including
xerography, photocopying and recording, or in any information storage
or retrieval system, is forbidden without the written permission of the
publisher, Harlequin Enterprises Limited, 225 Duncan Mill Road,
Don Mills, Ontario, Canada M3B 3K9.

This is a work of fiction. Names, characters, places and incidents are
either the product of the author's imagination or are used fictitiously,
and any resemblance to actual persons, living or dead, business
establishments, events or locales is entirely coincidental.

This edition published by arrangement with Harlequin Books S.A.

For questions and comments about the quality of this book
please contact us at Customer_eCare@Harlequin.ca.

® and TM are trademarks of the publisher. Trademarks indicated with
® are registered in the United States Patent and Trademark Office, the
Canadian Trade Marks Office and in other countries.

www.eHarlequin.com

Printed in U.S.A.

ABOUT THE AUTHOR

Tracy Wolff collects books, English degrees and lipsticks and has been known to forget where, and sometimes who, she is when immersed in a great novel. A writing and feminist literature professor at her local community college, she has spent years reading, teaching and writing about life as a woman in twenty-first-century America—with all its ups and downs. She is married to a wonderful man and is the mother of three terrific and rambunctious sons, who keep her on her toes. They make their home in Texas.

Books by Tracy Wolff

HARLEQUIN SUPERROMANCE

Don't miss any of our special offers. Write to us at the following address for information on our newest releases.

Harlequin Reader Service
U.S.: 3010 Walden Ave., P.O. Box 1325, Buffalo, NY 14269
Canadian: P.O. Box 609, Fort Erie, Ont. L2A 5X3

To Emily and Shellee
Thanks for all the fun,
friendship and collaboration

CHAPTER ONE

SHE COULD DO THIS.

She could do this.

Really, she *could* do *this*.

Rhiannon Jenkins repeated the mantra that had gotten her through so much in the past two years as she squared her shoulders and climbed slowly out of her car. Despite the pep talk she'd given herself all the way over here, she couldn't help feeling like she was headed for the guillotine. Which was ridiculous, she reminded herself impatiently. It was just a business lunch, and she'd had hundreds of them over the course of her career. One more certainly wasn't going to do her in.

Of course, she'd told herself the same thing three years before when she'd made the mistake of trusting a source for her newspaper article. That meeting hadn't killed her, but it had come damn close—and taken a huge amount of her life with it. Including, she admitted with a grim sigh, her ability to confidently meet a man in a packed restaurant—even for a lunch date that was strictly business.

But she didn't have a choice. She had to do this. The only other option—running back to her boss and best friend, Logan, and telling him that she'd been too chicken to even walk in the restaurant's door—was somehow a million times worse. He'd taken a chance on her when she'd been all but paralyzed with grief and fear. She wouldn't repay him by screwing up one of the biggest responsibilities he'd given her.

So what if it was the first time she'd pitched a party completely on her own since joining Logan's firm two years before?

So what if the man she was supposed to have lunch with was young and sexy and a little bit intimidating?

So what, even if she was so scared she was literally quaking in the two-hundred-dollar boots she'd bought the night before to give herself courage?

She could do this. She *would* do this…even if it sent her careening over the edge of the sanity she clung to with battered fingertips. She was never going to get better, never going to get any sort of a life back, if she didn't push herself. It was what she'd told Logan when he'd asked if doing this first meeting alone was really okay with her, and it was what she'd told herself in the bathroom mirror a hundred times that morning as she'd put on her makeup.

After gathering the briefcase and purse she'd almost forgotten in the car, Rhiannon headed straight toward the front door of the Mexican restaurant Shawn—the client—had chosen. As she walked, she did her best to banish the nerves that continued to assault her.

She'd spent her life around men—all kinds of men—so she felt ridiculous working herself up into this state just because he'd called the office and specifically requested her. *Why wouldn't he have?* she asked herself viciously. *She'd* been the one he'd met at the party she'd coordinated on Saturday night, and it was *her* business card she'd handed him when he'd asked what company she was with. It only stood to reason that he would have asked for her when he'd spoken to the receptionist two days before.

Understanding the whys of how she'd gotten there didn't make it any easier to open the restaurant's door and walk inside. But then, nothing had been easy for nearly three years now. That didn't mean she'd stopped doing things—it only meant that she had to go through this ridiculous freak-out in anticipation of every new or not-since-the-attack incident that came up. For a woman who had once been known for her intrepid and insightful newspaper articles, it was a hard thing for her to admit. And even harder for her to accept.

She spotted Shawn almost as soon as her eyes adjusted to the restaurant's dim interior—he was sitting in a booth about halfway across the room, and her first glimpse of him had Rhiannon silently cursing like a sailor.

She'd wanted to get here first, had made sure to arrive ten minutes early so that she'd have a chance to get herself settled at the table before having to put on her game face. The fact that her plans were now ruined flustered her a lot more than it should have.

Telling herself to suck it up, she returned his welcoming wave and made her way toward him. Even the best-laid plans had to have some wiggle room, she reminded herself as she stopped next to his table. Today, now, was no exception.

"Rhiannon." Shawn rose and extended his hand, his blue eyes warm and his smile welcoming. "I'm so glad you could make it today."

"Me, too. I've been excited about hearing the details

of this party you want to throw since you called the office on Monday." It wasn't a lie, she told herself, if she only told half the truth. She *was* excited about planning the party, so it was perfectly acceptable to leave out the fact that she'd been up half the night worrying about seeing him again.

Obviously, this was stupid, as he wasn't looking at her with anything more than polite interest—the same interest he would show any woman charged with creating a fantastic party so that he could impress a bunch of Hollywood types. She must have imagined the way he'd looked at her the other night—which wasn't much of a surprise. Her radar was way off when it came to men these days, and had been for much too long.

"I'm glad. I need someone who's excited about this thing, since I'm still trying to figure out how I feel about throwing a formal party."

She pulled out her laptop and booted it up so that she could take notes while they talked. "You don't like formal parties?" she asked, culling about half of the options she'd come up with that morning from the mental list she wanted to run by him.

"I'm more a beer-and-nachos kind of guy. But I figure if I'm going to do this, I need to do it right— formal, sit-down dinner, monkey suit, the works."

As if his way with words wasn't enough to clue her in, just looking at him gave her a good idea as to why the formal approach probably wasn't the way to go. With his shaggy brown hair and easy smile, Shawn Emerson looked like every footloose, slacker guy she'd ever run across—the kind who was more comfortable with a bat in one hand and a beer in the other than he ever would be in an office or behind a desk.

Even his meeting attire—a football jersey and a worn pair of jeans—screamed immature male out for a good time. It was just one of the many reasons she hated that her hand was still warm from where his had clasped it.

But then, she was an idiot when it came to men. Life had certainly proven that in the past three years.

"So, your usual party style is ultra-casual yet you're thinking about throwing a completely formal gathering?"

"It's actually my agent's idea. He thinks I should have a really impressive gathering, kind of knock those Hollywood types' socks off. I'm just trying to follow along with his suggestions."

"What's the occasion?" she asked, trying to gauge which direction he really wanted to go in. For some people, formal meant black tie, while for others, it was just a step or two above beach attire. She had him pegged for the latter.

"Endeavor Studios just optioned the rights to my graphic novels. They're rushing to write a script based on the first two with hopes of starting filming in about eighteen months if everything goes as planned. A bunch of the guys involved in buying my project are going to be here in Austin for the film festival in March, debuting a new movie and Anthony thinks I should have a no-holds-barred party to welcome them to Austin and show my appreciation. It's not every day a guy's told his character is going to be made into a major motion-picture franchise, after all."

So much for a step above bathing suits—she'd been wrong again. Big surprise. This guy was definitely in need of a party with a big wow factor.

But a huge Hollywood-style party meant pulling out all the stops and the film festival was only—she pulled the website up on her computer—six weeks away. He wanted her to do a major party like this in *six weeks?* Was he kidding?

Trying to get her thoughts straight, Rhiannon pulled up a list of questions she needed to ask, then turned to him with the first one. "Who is Shadeslayer?"

Shawn grinned, an excited, happy smile lighting up his whole face and causing a weird flip-flopping in the pit of her stomach. Rhiannon did her best to ignore the feeling—the guy was at least ten years younger than her—probably closer to fifteen. Just the idea that his smile was directed at her specifically was absurd, not to mention pathetic.

"I was hoping you'd ask." He reached down to the seat beside him and picked up a few thick comic-book-style novels that he slapped on the table between them. "He's the superhero I created when I was in college. Now, he's the star of my twice-yearly graphic novels."

She blinked at the garish covers staring up at her. All three had a strong, muscle-bound guy in a gray-and-black superhero suit looking out of them, although he was in a different kind of peril on each cover. The artwork was absolutely gorgeous, but— "You write comic books for a living?"

"Graphic novels. It's not quite the same thing."

"Right, of course." She couldn't help wondering what the difference was, but didn't want to ask, in case the question offended him. He had made a point of correcting her when she'd called them comic books, after all. "What does Shadeslayer *do?*"

"All kinds of things, but mainly he keeps shades—dead people who are trapped on Earth—from using their powers to enslave humans." He held the books out to her. "Here, take them. They're for you. I figured they'd give you a sense of who I am, what the deal was about."

"Oh, okay. That's very nice of you." She reached out to take the books, her hand trembling just a little as it brushed against his.

She had no idea what she was supposed to do with three comic books, but it was a sweet gesture. She opened the cover of the first one, began to flip through it and was shocked when she came to the title page. Scrawled between the title and his name, were the words, "To Rhiannon, because a party is so often just the beginning. Shawn Emerson."

She stared at the inscription a moment, unsure what to make of it. Were the words a threat? A promise? A suggestion? Her back stiffened and she closed the books without comment, even as she tried desperately to figure out Shawn's agenda.

"Do you like them?" he asked, and she looked up to find him watching her closely.

"Of course I do," she answered, ignoring the confusion inside that told her very clearly that she wasn't sure how she felt about the books—or about the man who had given them to her. "They're an interesting gift."

Interesting? Nice? SHAWN barely suppressed a shudder. Obviously, he'd struck out big time with his gift—he'd been an idiot to think Rhiannon would be interested in his graphic novels. He almost hadn't brought them—he didn't give them away very often anymore, and rarely

signed them now that he was no longer busting his ass
on self-sponsored book tours to promote the things—
but this morning he'd been struck by a sudden desire
to show her what he did. To give her a glimpse of
himself, and of Shadeslayer, the greatest character he'd
ever created.

But from the way she placed the books on the table
like they were a cross between poison ivy and rot-
ting meat, he figured he probably should have gone
with flowers instead—for some reason, women always
seemed to like those more. Leaning back in his chair,
he studied Rhiannon and tried to decide what kind of
flower she was.

Not a rose, though she was long-stemmed, beautiful
and surprisingly fragile, if the delicate hand she'd put
in his was any indication.

Not a daisy, because she was much too quiet and self-
possessed for the cheerful white-and-yellow flowers.

Carnations were boring, and while she was doing
her best to blend into the woodwork in her bland gray
suit and white blouse, he had a feeling she was anything
but boring underneath. Not with those intense coffee-
colored eyes and that fiery red hair.

No, carnations would never do—and neither would
orchids. They were too temperamental. Which left him
drawing a blank. He shoved the dilemma to the back
of his mind, with a quick reminder to get back to it
later after they'd talked more. Because he'd meant what
he'd said when he'd signed those books—this party
was just the beginning. He'd been thinking about her
since they'd met Saturday night and couldn't wait for
a chance to get to know her.

The waitress chose that moment to come up for

their orders, and he watched as Rhiannon smoothed a self-conscious hand over the tight bun of her hair. He wondered if she ever let it down.

"You know, they make a killer margarita here. I'm partial to their plain ones, but Lissa swears by their sangria margaritas." He deliberately brought up the name of his best friend Robert's wife to put her at ease—Lissa was the one who had introduced them at the party the other night, and it had been obvious she and Rhiannon liked each other very much. "I swear, she can drink three or four of those in a sitting."

She stared at him. "It's one o'clock in the afternoon."

"One-fifteen, actually," he corrected her, reaching for a chip.

"Either way." Her voice was drier than the martinis his mother used to make—and gulp down by the half dozen. "I try not to drink during business hours."

"Right. Business. I can see that about you."

That got her attention. She looked away from the waitress, eyebrows furrowed, lips pulled into a deep frown. "What's that supposed to mean?"

"Nothing. Just that you seem like a really *responsible* person." He barely succeeded in hiding his grin as Rhiannon's teeth snapped together with an all but audible click.

"Well, we can't all have the intellectual and emotional makeup of a thirteen-year-old boy. More's the pity."

"Touché." He inclined his head, offering her the verbal point. As he did, he let his eyes linger on her full upper lip and the dimple that kept flirting with her left cheek. He'd been fascinated with both from the first time he'd seen her—and the story they told.

Even at the party, she'd looked so prim and proper. Long sleeves, long skirt, blouse buttoned up to her throat. He'd wondered at first if she was channeling someone's maiden aunt. But then she'd opened her mouth and that voice—low and smoky and incredibly sexy—had curled around him. And he'd wondered how he could have ever failed to see the fire.

He saw it now, as she turned to the waitress and ordered a glass of water with a twist of lime. Plain, boring, expected—with just a little kick to keep things interesting. It was that little kick, all those tiny contradictions, that had had him calling her in the first place.

Yes, he needed a party planner, but the artist in him—who was he kidding, the *man* in him—wanted to unravel her a bit. To see what was underneath the sensible shoes and simple pearl earrings. To see if she lived up to the promise of that voice, that hair and the incredible body she kept so tightly under wraps.

He ordered a beer, and then settled back to study her while she looked over the menu. He couldn't help himself. She was a series of stops and goes that would probably drive a normal man crazy. But he was a far cry from normal and he'd always loved a puzzle. There was just something cool about piecing together bits and pieces of a person until he had the whole picture assembled.

Rhiannon was one hell of a picture and one hell of a puzzle. It would be a lot of fun finding out how all her contradictions, all her jagged pieces, fit together.

After all, the journey was always so much more fun than the destination.

"See anything you like?" he asked after silence had stretched between them for several minutes. When she didn't immediately answer, he reached out and trailed a finger down the back of her hand.

Those brown eyes flew up from the menu to meet his, a hint of temper flaring in their depths as she very deliberately moved her hand away. He filed away the knowledge that she didn't like to be touched—at least not by business acquaintances—and waited for her to answer.

"I was thinking of the *pollo diablo,*" she answered as she set her menu aside. "It was delicious the last time I came here."

He couldn't stop the grin that spread across his face. The most buttoned-up woman in the place was ordering the spiciest dish on the menu. Oh, yes, unraveling her layers would be a huge challenge. One he was suddenly looking forward to very much.

CHAPTER TWO

AFTER THEY'D ORDERED, Shawn watched as Rhiannon made a concerted effort to get the business meeting back on track. There was no more talk about margaritas or spicy food or whether or not she was a responsible person, but that was okay with him. He had time. Planning this party was going to take weeks, and he planned on being *very* involved in the details.

"So, according to their website, the film festival is in town from Wednesday through Sunday of the last week in March," said Rhiannon as she surfed the Net, no longer even bothering to look at him. "What night were you thinking of having the party?"

He wondered if he should be offended that she appeared to have so little interest in him, when most women went out of their way to attract him—and his Shadeslayer fortune. But he found her attitude kind of refreshing, especially since the thing she was focused so intently on was his party, and therefore still related to him.

He hadn't been joking when he'd said that his parties tended toward the spur of the moment and ultra-casual. The most planning he ever put in was picking up the phone and dialing half a dozen of his friends a couple hours before a game started. Which meant if he was going to do this thing right—the way his agent wanted it done—he was going to need all the advice she could give him.

"Probably Thursday night. Friday and Saturday nights are booked with premieres and industry parties." He grabbed a chip, popped it in his mouth.

"Okay." She clicked a few computer keys, adding that information to some database, he presumed.

"For how many people?"

"I don't know. What do you suggest?"

She raised an eyebrow at him over the laptop screen. "I don't know who's going to be in town or how many of them you want to impress. If you could give me a ballpark figure, I could get an idea of the best way to put the party together."

"Sure." In his head, he went over the list his agent had given him and then added a number of his friends in town. "Probably about a hundred people, give or take."

"Okay. So you said Thursday night, but there are screenings going on until ten o'clock. Do you want a late supper, after the showings are over?"

"That's what I was planning on. But you don't sound all that enthusiastic."

"No, that kind of party would be lovely—"

"But?"

"But I think that it'll blend into the hundreds of other parties that your VIP guests have been to."

"That's the last thing I want. I want to do something they'll remember, something that will stand out later from their week here. Something that will really rock."

"Well, then you're going to have to step outside your comfort zone. Or into it, as the case may be."

"I like the sound of *that*." He grinned at her.

She took a sip of her water and went back to perusing the film festival's website, ignoring his smile. Which, of course, only made him more determined than ever to get her attention.

Part of him felt like he was back in elementary school, pulling the pigtails of Mary Louise Elkins, the girl who had sat in front of him every year from kindergarten through fifth grade. It had driven her nuts, but he hadn't been able to help it—negative attention from her had been way better than no attention at all.

He paused at the realization, a chip halfway to his mouth. Maybe Rhiannon was right about his emotional development being slightly arrested. He should probably work on that if he expected her to see him as more than a potential client.

"So you've told me the kind of party you usually throw. What's your favorite kind of party to attend?" Rhiannon asked, finally setting the laptop aside.

"Same thing—beer, chips, football. It's all good."

"Well, if that's really the case, why are we throwing such a fancy party? Why don't we throw one you might actually enjoy?"

He laughed. "It's March—no football."

"That's not what I meant. What if you throw a really relaxed party—jeans, casual food, games. It would be totally different than they're used to, and it could be a lot of fun."

"What, you mean, like a barbecue?"

"I don't know, I haven't gotten that far yet. But a barbecue could work."

"I know it's a sin to live in the South and say this,

but I'm not a big fan of charred meat and potato salad. The whole barbecue culture gene kind of passed me by."

"You know, barbecue doesn't have to mean beans and brisket next to an open fire. A good steak could be classified as barbecue."

He shook his head. "That's not really my point. Changing the type of meat served doesn't change the barbecue culture. I'm not into it."

"All right then. I get it. No barbecue." She went back to the computer, clicked a few times. "So are you opposed to the idea of a casual party altogether, or just one that involves 'charred meat and potato salad'?"

He was about to shoot her idea down in its entirety, though it pained him to do so—in his experience, women weren't at their friendliest after a man told them he thought their plans were less than impressive. And there was little he wanted more than to have Rhiannon in a friendly mood.

But her idea was so far from what he'd been thinking—and from what Anthony expected—that he didn't feel like he had a choice. But then she turned the computer around and pointed to a couple of menus that were as far from a typical Texas barbecue as you could get, but that were a lot more interesting than the fancy hors d'oeuvres he was used to getting at parties like the one his agent expected him to throw.

"You can do gourmet pizzas on the grill?" he asked skeptically.

"Caterers can do just about anything on a grill these days—including dessert. Don't you ever watch the Food channel?"

"I don't, no. I'm more partial to movies myself. Give me a good horror movie and I'm happy."

Her smile was slow coming, but when it finally arrived, he'd felt as if he'd scaled Mount Everest. It was a real smile, one that warmed her eyes and brought her dimple out in full force, and it made him happy just to watch how it lit up her face. He had a feeling Rhiannon didn't smile much—at least not out of genuine amusement. It felt good to be the one to put a smile on her face.

"I'm partial to slasher films myself."

"Oh, yeah? Which ones?" He felt his curiosity pique. It was the first personal bit of information Rhiannon had revealed about herself.

She named a couple of movies he'd enjoyed enough to buy on DVD, and they spent the next few minutes talking about them—debating level of gruesomeness and special effects and story line. Rhiannon was surprisingly knowledgeable about the genre, which made him wonder if he'd misread her reaction to his novels. Any woman who liked the films she did also had to be partial to a good superhero story. That same suspension of disbelief was a requirement for any true action movie fan.

He was about to invite her to a movie that was opening on Friday night when she once again steered the conversation back to business. "So, if I come up with a casual menu that is also impressive, will you consider having a less formal event?"

"Sure. If you can come up with a really great idea, one that's fun and casual and impressive all at the same time, we'll try your route."

"Fun, casual and impressive all at the same time, hmm? You don't ask for much."

"Oh, Rhiannon." He shook his head, shooting her a wicked grin. "I've barely gotten started on the list of demands I have for you."

SHE NEARLY CHOKED on her water. As it was, the slightly tangy liquid went down the wrong pipe, burning from the back of her throat all the way to her lungs. Her eyes watered and her chest ached, but she did everything she could not to cough—it *so* wouldn't do to let Shawn know how blatantly he affected her. He was already cocky and charming and full of mischief—the last thing she wanted was to encourage him.

Liar, a little voice inside of her said. There was a small part of her that wanted to do exactly that, that wanted to say to hell with logic and responsibility and fear. God knew, he'd been flirting with her since she'd sat down. Would it be so terrible if she responded in kind? It's not like the world would end if she showed some interest.

The very thought robbed Rhiannon of her recently recovered breath, had her heart beating in a stressed-out syncopation. Who was she kidding? She could barely handle meeting new clients in the middle of a bustling party—how did she think she'd manage flirting with a gorgeous, younger man when the two of them were on their own?

It was too absurd to even contemplate.

And if her baggage wasn't bad enough, trying to step out of her self-imposed cocoon with a man whose event could spark a rush of business for Parties by L.K. was just asking for trouble. When it went bad, when she quickly made a total and complete fool of herself because she couldn't handle the pressure—and there was little doubt in her mind that she would freak out eventually—how humiliating would it be to still have to see him? To still have to work with him and pretend that she was anything but the basket case she was? Or worse, to run into him at other parties. The upper-crust Austin social scene was a relatively small one, and she really didn't want to spend the next few months worrying about whether or not Shawn was going to be at one of the events she was planning.

She drew a couple discreet breaths in through her nose, praying he wouldn't notice her distress—or the pain that was ripping through her upper torso because she was too stubborn to cough. He didn't say a word as she struggled, and she began to hope he hadn't noticed how he'd affected her. But when she finally made it on the road to recovery, it was to find Shawn watching her with amusement. "You okay there?"

So much for discretion. Was it too much to ask to sink through the floor before she died of total and complete humiliation?

"Fine, thanks." Her eyes were still watering and her voice was hoarse, but at least she'd gotten the words out.

"Good. I'd really hate for something to happen to you before the big night." He winked, and as she stared into his wicked blue eyes, she suddenly wasn't at all sure he was still talking about the party.

"I can take care of myself."

"I never meant to imply that you couldn't."

"So, Shawn." Rhiannon took a deep breath and contemplated the best way to steer the conversation back toward the party. "Have you thought about what venue you want to use? Austin has a number of great places—"

"I just figured we'd use my house. It's plenty big."

"For a hundred people to mingle comfortably?" Where did the man live? The only houses in Austin big enough for that were on the Lake, and surely his graphic novels didn't pay enough to make that a reality—

"I've got two acres on Lake Travis. I bought it a couple years ago as an investment, but it's a perfect place to entertain. The house is huge and there's a gigantic yard that overlooks the lake."

Two acres? On Lake Travis? Obviously the graphic novel business was a much better proposition than she had ever imagined—even before the film rights. She thought of her own fifteen-hundred-square-foot condo, of how she'd struggled to pay for it after the divorce a couple of years before. Amazing to think that a man who was so much younger than she was had already achieved so much. Amazing and disheartening. But then, starting over at close to forty often was.

Richard had offered to help her, but by the time the divorce had been finalized, she'd wanted nothing from him. Nothing from any man. It still amazed her that he'd been able to just walk away from their fifteen-year marriage, as if everything they'd built together—everything they'd meant to each other—had never existed. Sometimes when she was lying in bed at night, staring at the ceiling and praying for the insomnia to go away, she wondered if he'd left—if he hadn't been able to deal—because she'd gotten too good at playing the victim. But with family and friends crowding in from every side, it had been hard to be anything else.

"So, do you want to see it?"

Shawn's words interrupted her self-castigation and she looked at him blankly as the words sunk in.

"See it?"

"My house? Maybe it could help you get a feel for the best way to do this party."

"I thought you said on the phone you didn't have time to run back home today. If you want to take me back to your house, why did we bother meeting here to begin with?"

"So I could buy you lunch." He reached over and nicked the check the waitress had dropped onto the edge of the table as she passed by.

"You don't have to do that. You're the client." She held her hand out for the bill. "It's my responsibility to—"

"Do you always play by the rules?"

It was on the tip of her tongue to say no, that for long years she'd barely paid attention to the fact that there *were* rules, but instead, said, "Yes. It's safer that way."

"Safer." He lifted an eyebrow.

"Better," she amended hastily. "It's *better* that way." She tugged self-consciously at the long sleeve of her shirt.

He threw a couple of twenties down on the table, then stood. He held out a hand to her. "Come on, let's go to my place. I'll show you my gazebo."

"Is that an updated version of the old etchings line?" she asked as they walked toward the front door.

The look he shot her was brimming with laughter. "You caught me."

"Yes, well, I'm throwing you back. I've got another

appointment in less than an hour, so I can't run all the way out to the lake right now."

"Another appointment? Are you cheating on me already?"

"Yes, with a tall, blond lawyer who has a corporate expense account." As soon as the words were out of her mouth, she wanted to take them back. There was no use encouraging him and his flirtatious behavior. Not when it couldn't go anywhere.

"Beaten out by a lawyer? I'm not sure how I'll survive that indignity."

"I'm sure you'll muddle through somehow."

"Can I see you again?"

Her heart skipped a beat, then crashed against her ribs. She ignored it—and the terror racing through her. "Of course. We're working on this party together, aren't we?"

"That's not what I meant." He took a step closer, until his body was only a few inches from hers. She didn't move away. "But you already knew that."

"I did." *What am I doing?* she wondered, shocked at her odd behavior. *What the hell am I doing?*

"Come to my house on Friday. I'll show you around, take you down to the lake."

"I have appointments all day—and a party at night."

"Saturday, then." His eyes were darker than they'd been earlier, a deep sapphire-blue that seemed to see into the very heart of her. But that was impossible. No one had gotten in her head for longer than she could remember. It was absurd to think that this man, this *boy*—with his ready smile and silly banter—had been able to do so after one lunch.

"Saturday is our busy day. I've got a morning brunch and than an afternoon garden party."

"Come later then."

"I probably won't get out of the last event until after seven."

"How will I manage to stay awake that late?" he teased. "Come on, Rhiannon. The sooner you see the house, the sooner you can decide what kind of party to have. Come see me Saturday night."

"It'll be too dark to see the grounds."

"There's this great, newfangled invention called electricity. Surely you've heard of it? My backyard is wired better than the landing strips at the airport." His smile was bigger now, as if he was just waiting for her next objection so he could shoot it down, too.

Charmed despite herself, Rhiannon smiled. "Okay, fine. You've convinced me. Saturday night at seven-thirty."

"Excellent. Our second date—I can't wait."

"Second date?"

He took another step toward her and suddenly she couldn't breathe.

"This was business." She forced the words out through a throat so tight she had to fight for air. "And so is our appointment on Saturday."

"We had food, flirtatious banter, fun. Feels like a date to me."

"I drove myself, researched the film festival on my computer, and any flirtatious banter was completely one-sided. Feels more like a business meeting to me."

He reached out, stroked his hand softly down her cheek. As he did, she could feel the calluses on his fingers from years of drawing. "And this?" he asked as his thumb smoothed over her lips. "What does this feel like?"

She was still struggling for an answer when he leaned in and his lips brushed, but just barely, against her own.

CHAPTER THREE

"HEY, BEAUTIFUL. How'd the consult go?" Rhiannon looked up from her computer in time to see Logan Kelly breeze into her office with a cup of coffee in each hand and curiosity rife in his gaze. "Did you nail it?"

"I think so. He wants to meet Saturday after the Henderson event so that I can see his house. He thinks it will make the perfect venue for the party. Which he wants to have during the big film festival."

"That's only six weeks away—how big of a party are we talking about?"

"A hundred people, with full-scale entertainment and food."

"That's a pretty big order, Rhiannon. You sure you can handle it on your own?"

No, she wasn't even close to being sure she could handle it. But she was determined to anyway. She owed it to Logan to step up to the plate—after all, he was one of the few people who'd been willing to take a risk on her when she'd wanted to change careers after almost fifteen years as a journalist.

Since she'd joined his firm nearly two years before, he'd been giving her the simple jobs, letting her ease back into the world at the speed she was comfortable with. But she was getting pretty good at the whole event-planning thing and she wanted to try her hand at something bigger—something like Shawn's party. Besides, she couldn't hide behind what had happened to her forever. The rape had taken almost everything from her—her husband, her career, her sense of self. She wasn't going to let it take her professional pride, too. It was the only thing she had left.

She forced a smile. "I can do it. After all, I've been watching you make the impossible happen for a year now."

"And flattery will get you everywhere." He settled into the chair across from hers and took a long sip from his coffee. "So, where's his house?"

"On Lake Travis. He says he's got two acres up there."

"Seriously?" Logan let out a long whistle. "Who is this guy? Some rich Austinite looking to break into Hollywood?"

"Not quite. Actually, he already got that break. He just sold film rights to his novels or something."

"Really? What's his name?"

"Shawn Emerson. I've never heard of him, but obviously someone in Hollywood has—"

"No way! Shawn Emerson? Of Shadeslayer fame?"

Rhiannon stared at him, shocked. "Yeah. He mentioned Shadeslayer while we were at lunch today. Have you read any of the books?"

"Are you kidding me? I've read them all. Shadeslayer's one of the greatest superheroes ever written. Surely you've seen him somewhere. He's a really dark hero, dresses all in gray and black, including his mask. Walks a thin line between right and wrong."

"Yeah, no, pretty sure I'd never heard of him before today." She reached into her purse and pulled out the books Shawn had given her. "You're talking about these comic books, right?"

"They're graphic novels, not comic books. There's a big difference."

"So I keep hearing." She watched in amusement as Logan picked up the top book with uncharacteristic awe. "Is this what I think it is?" he asked reverently.

"I don't know. What do you think it is?"

"A first edition of *Shadeslayer's Revenge*." He opened the cover. "Signed! Do you have any idea how much this is worth?"

"Not a clue."

"A lot—I bet you could get a few thousand for it easy on eBay."

"Seriously? For a comic book? I mean, I understand Spiderman or Batman, but this is some new hero no one's ever heard of."

"A lot of people have heard of him. And I told you, it's not a comic book. Graphic novels are kind of a cross between regular novels and comic books. Shadeslayer has been around for five or six years now, with two books coming out each year. There's a huge Slayer counterculture that gets really excited every time a new book is set to come out."

"And you're not part of that counterculture?" she asked archly.

"No. I mean, yeah, I buy his books as soon as they hit the shelves, but I don't dress up like characters from the books or anything."

"And for that, I'm sure we're all grateful."

Logan ignored her. "So, when is the movie coming out? Will there be a sequel? Which book are they scripting? How many—"

"Whoa!" Rhiannon felt like she'd fallen into an alternate universe. "Does your wife know about this little obsession of yours?"

"Sandy likes the books, too. So does Mike."

"Well, I can understand how Mike would. Your kid's twelve years old. But you're nearly forty."

"Hey, I'm the same age as you."

"Exactly my point. You don't see me going gaga over some comic-book character."

"*Graphic novel* character, thank you very much." He grinned.

"Oh, excuse me."

"I don't know if you should be excused. You managed to land this guy when I'd give my left arm to work with him." Logan flipped open the second book, then the third, pausing when he got to the dedication Shawn had written for Rhiannon.

He stopped flipping pages and pinned her with a look that made her flush immediately. Gone was the aging fan boy and in his place was her too-shrewd best friend. "What's going on, Rhiannon?"

"Nothing."

"This doesn't sound like nothing. 'The party's just the beginning?' Is he bothering you?"

"No. It's nothing like that."

"Nothing like what?" Logan's eyes narrowed dangerously. "Has he come on to you?"

"Of course not."

"Why don't I believe that?"

"Because you're the most suspicious man I've ever met?"

"No, that's not it. Maybe it's because you're the worst liar *I've* ever met. You keep twirling your pencil in your hair—that's a dead giveaway. You do it only when you're nervous. Or lying."

She slammed the pencil she was holding onto the desk, nearly yanking a chunk of her hair out in the process. "I am not lying. He didn't do anything overt. I just got the impression that he was…interested. But I don't know. My radar's all screwed up when it comes to men. You know that—"

"Your radar is just fine," Logan said firmly. "One minor mistake doesn't mean you can't trust your instincts."

"I wouldn't exactly call it minor."

"You know what I mean. None of that was your fault, Rhiannon."

"Look, I don't want to talk about it. This whole conversation is ridiculous. I mean, he's obviously famous, and probably rich—"

"Definitely rich."

She ignored him. "Plus he's younger than I am, by at least five years."

"More like ten or twelve—"

"You're not helping."

"Sorry." He held up his hands, as if in surrender.

"Well, actually, maybe you are. Why would some twenty-some-year-old guy be interested in *me?*" Rhiannon breathed a sigh of relief, her stomach muscles unknotting as she allowed herself to be convinced by her own words, despite the kiss. "He wouldn't. So it's no big deal, then. I was just reading the signals wrong."

"Not to ruin the peace you seem to have found, but have you looked in a mirror lately?"

She stiffened, tried not to react to his words. She reminded herself that Logan meant them in a good way, but that didn't seem to matter. Not when the answer was no—she hadn't looked in a mirror. Not for years, or at least not for any longer than it took to apply a quick coat of lipstick and mascara before a party.

She was too afraid of what she might see.

"You're a beautiful woman, Rhiannon."

"Does your wife know you go around saying things like that to other women?" she asked, trying to divert his attention.

"Sandy agrees with me. She tells me regularly we should try to find someone to fix you up with."

"Logan, no!"

"Relax, I'm not trying to get you to go out on a blind date. I wouldn't do that. I just brought it up so you'd know that it's not far-fetched that this guy could be interested in you."

"I don't want him to be interested in me."

"Well, then, don't worry about it." Logan drained the last of his coffee, setting the cup on her desk like he always did. For two years now, he'd been making coffee and bringing her a cup, with the tacit understanding that she was in charge of cleanup. Since she made terrible coffee the situation worked perfectly for both of them. "If he makes a move on you, shoot him down. That should be enough to send him packing. And if it doesn't, I'll take over the account. It'd be no hardship for me to work with the genius who created Shadeslayer. As it is, I'm more than a little jealous that you get to."

"Yeah, well, feel free to take over anytime."

"Believe me, I would." He headed for the door. "But somehow, I think Emerson would notice the last-minute substitution. My legs just aren't nearly as good as yours." He ducked out of the door just as the stress balls she kept on her desk went sailing across the room, smacking the door frame exactly where his head had been only moments before.

CHAPTER FOUR

FOR WHAT HAD TO BE the fifth time in as many minutes, Shawn stirred the pasta sauce he'd spent the better half of his afternoon making. Rhiannon was late. Not stand-him-up-late, or even kind-of-rude late—at least, not yet. But still, the seconds were crawling by, probably because he'd spent all day counting down to seven-thirty, only to have it come and go with no fanfare whatsoever.

Lifting the wooden spoon to his lips, Shawn tasted his maternal grandmother's pasta sauce with a grin. Like always, it was delicious. He'd have to tell her so the next time they spoke.

He glanced at the clock. Seven forty-five. She'd probably just gotten hung up at the party—it was her job to take care of things, after all. Besides, normally he wouldn't even notice if his date was late—he'd be too engrossed in working on the latest adventures of Shadeslayer. But he hadn't been able to write a word or draw a picture all day—he'd been too busy thinking about Rhiannon.

It was ridiculous, really, how excited he was about this date. He'd dated a lot of women through the years—since Cynthia had died, he'd made it a point not to get serious about any of them—so he couldn't figure out why he was getting so worked up this time. Over this woman.

Sure, she was beautiful, but he'd learned long ago that beauty was often only skin deep. Cynthia had been absolutely gorgeous, yet when they'd been engaged, she'd made his life a living hell for longer than he cared to remember.

No, it wasn't Rhiannon's looks he was responding to so strongly. Maybe it was her cautious sense of humor, the one she kept hidden but that came out at the best moments? Or the fact that she was extremely cautious, yet had chosen to come here anyway. She might look fragile, she might even *be* fragile, but she was braver than he'd first given her credit for. And that he admired the hell out of her for.

The ringing of his doorbell had him all but leaping over the counter. Telling himself to chill—or he really would scare her away—Shawn headed through the entryway to the front door. He pulled it open, and couldn't stop the smile that stretched across his face.

She looked good—really good—all dressed up from the afternoon garden party in a long-sleeved wrap-dress of navy silk. Her briefcase was slung over her shoulder and though he caught tantalizing glimpses of cleavage as she stepped inside, it was her smile that really caught his attention. Wide and happy, it transformed her whole face from sedately beautiful to breathtaking. If he looked closely, he could even see that small, peekaboo dimple in her left cheek. It made her look like a teenager.

"I'm sorry I'm late. The party ran long, and then the caterers took forever to clean up. Which ended up being nice, actually, because it gave the client plenty of time to gush about how great the party was. Seven of the guests walked away with my business card, promising to call early next week." She laughed, a sweet, tinkling sound he'd never heard from her before. Which was a shame—she had a great laugh, though it sounded a little rusty, and it bugged him that she usually held herself back so much.

"Believe me, I understand how work can wreak havoc on the best-laid plans." He rested a light hand on her lower back as he ushered her through to the kitchen. "I have a tendency to get lost in my own world when I'm working."

"You don't have to tell me that. I know all about you artistic types."

Something dangerous flashed inside him, something he couldn't name. Jealousy, maybe, that she'd been with some artistic type before him? But that was stupid—it wasn't like there was anything between them. Yet. Still, he couldn't resist asking, "Really? And how is it you're so intimately acquainted with us artistic types?"

She paused at his tone, and he watched as her normal reserve came back. He could have kicked himself. "My whole family has an artistic bent of one type or another," she said, all traces of levity gone. "My oldest brother's an architect now, but when he was younger he had visions of being a great *artiste*. My mother was amazed he made it through adolescence without chopping off an ear."

"His own or someone else's?"

She inclined her head. "Either or. Matt was a handful when he was young."

"Do you have any other siblings?" he asked, watching her look around his kitchen in admiration. It was stupid, but he felt his chest swell at the thought that she so obviously liked something that was such an intrinsic part of him.

"Twin sisters, who are also younger than I. One designs jewelry and the other designs clothes."

"And you plan parties."

Something flickered in her eyes. "Yes, not very artistic of me I must admit, but it pays the bills nicely. I figure that's something."

"It is," he agreed, as he gestured for her to sit at the bar that ran along the center island of the kitchen.

"You're cooking!" She stared at the stove as if she'd never seen one before. "You really didn't have to do that."

"I figured you'd be hungry after going from one party to another today." He poured some pasta into the pot of water boiling on the stove. "Have you already eaten?"

"Yes, I—" She shook her head at the skeptical look he shot her. "No, I haven't. Not since my cup of yogurt this morning, anyway. I'd planned to grab something on the way here, but I was running late and didn't want to be any later."

"I could have waited a few more minutes, Rhiannon. But I'm glad you didn't eat—it's always nicer to cook for someone else."

"It smells delicious."

"It tastes even better. It's an old family recipe." He stirred the pasta sauce, then held the wooden spoon up to her lips. "Here, try."

At first he thought she was going to refuse, but right before he lowered the spoon, she leaned forward and took a tentative lick, her eyes widening as she tasted the tangy mix of tomatoes, garlic and fresh herbs. "That's really good." She took another, bigger bite.

"You don't have to sound so surprised."

"I'm sorry. It's just, I'm not used to men who can cook that well."

"You must be hanging out with the wrong kind of men."

"You have no idea." A shadow passed across her face, turning her already serious expression almost sad. Her brown eyes flickered and grew darker, and he couldn't help wondering what had happened to her that had put that look on her face.

It set off an alarm deep inside him, had him thinking that maybe he should take a step back. Reserved was one thing, but the last thing he really needed was to get involved with another woman who was damaged. Surviving Cynthia had nearly killed him.

The first awkward silence of the night descended as he popped the garlic bread in the oven. He waited for her to say something, but she didn't, and the stillness stretched from awkward to downright uncomfortable.

"I'm no whiz, but I can follow my grandmother's recipe pretty well," he commented in an effort to get things back on track. "She's a genius in the kitchen."

"Evidently." She grabbed on to the verbal life preserver with both hands. "But you're obviously no slouch, if that sauce is any indication."

"Thanks. Dinner will be ready in about fifteen minutes. Can I get you a drink while we wait?" He gestured to the bottle of red wine he had resting on the counter.

"Actually, a glass of water would be great. I'm parched from all the talking I had to do today."

"Sure." He filled a glass, handed it to her.

"I'd love to see your backyard—get a chance to look at the space."

"Absolutely." He led them through the family room toward the back door that would take them out to the large deck he and Robert had built the summer before last.

"Wow." She glanced around the huge room, with its cinema-sized television and state-of-the-art sound system. "This is a great room for a party, too." She wandered over to one of the arcade-sized pinball machines he had lined up against the side wall, ran a hand over it and took in the adventures of various famous superheroes painted on its sides.

"You really take this whole comic-book thing seriously, don't you?"

"Graphic novels, and yeah, I do. Seeing as how it's my job, I figure I'd better take it seriously."

"I'm sorry," she said. "I didn't mean to offend you."

"Don't worry. I'm not that easy to offend." He smiled at her, then changed the subject back to the party. "Most of the downstairs can be used—it's a giant circle, so all the rooms pretty much flow into one another."

He flipped on the outdoor lights as he opened the door, gestured for her to precede him, then waited for her reaction. He didn't have long to wait.

"Oh, my God, this is unbelievable. When you said you had two acres up here, I figured most of it would be wild and unusable. But this—" She held her arms out wide. "This is perfect. You could have twice as many people as we planned out here and still not be crowded."

"You want to go explore?" He nodded toward the well-lit path that curved from the deck through the entire yard.

"Try and stop me."

RHIANNON FELT A LITTLE like Alice in Wonderland as she combed through Shawn's yard. Everywhere she looked there was something else to see—a tall, intricately carved gazebo that would comfortably seat twelve. An abundant rose garden with benches scattered throughout. Hidden alcove after hidden alcove, each perfect for a food station or intimate seating arrangement. And then there was the gigantic pool, hot tub and basketball court that took up a significant portion of the backyard near the wrought-iron fence, not to mention the view of the lake, which, even at night, was breathtaking.

When Logan had talked about Shawn having money, she'd assumed he meant normal money. Reasonable money. Not holy-cow-he-lives-like-a-pasha-on-his-own-estate money. All this before the movies for his superhero had even come out? Obviously, she'd severely underestimated the graphic-novel market.

It was disconcerting on a personal level, especially considering the fact that he'd called this their second date and had made her dinner. After talking to him at the restaurant and finding out what he did for a living, she'd managed to convince herself that he was just a little boy in a man's body. She'd actually been happy about that—her unwitting attraction would die quickly under such circumstances.

She looked around the grounds. While all the toys and other things he'd had built made it obvious he liked to play, it was also becoming very clear that there was a lot more to Shawn than she'd originally thought. He had a beautiful, thoughtfully designed house, a career that he was obviously brilliant at and, despite it all, he was completely un-self-absorbed.

Most of the men she knew would have spent the whole time showing off the house, bragging about every little thing. But Shawn seemed more interested in learning about her than he did about impressing her. It was a little frightening, particularly since she found herself intrigued by his restraint.

It had been a long time since she'd been this interested in a man, and she didn't know what to make of it, didn't know how to act. Didn't know, even, if she wanted to be interested. It was an odd conundrum to be in.

He wasn't the first man to show interest in her since the attack, and he probably wouldn't be the last. Normally she was overwhelmed by panic at the thought of a man's attention and did her best to ignore them until they went away. She didn't like the way they made her feel—afraid, helpless, hopeless and overwhelmed by doubts that she would ever be normal again.

She didn't want to ignore Shawn. She didn't have a clue what she did want to do with him, but she knew that she didn't want to do that. Which was a problem in and of itself. Her old therapist would probably tell her that she'd chosen to be interested in him because he was safe. Unattainable.

Besides being way too young for her, he was also a client—at least, for the next six weeks. And the last thing she wanted was to get involved with a client. If she froze up, turned down his advances because she couldn't handle them, it would be awful to still have to show up and do his party. Of course, it would be even more awful if he took his business somewhere else.

No, it was better if she kept these odd little twinges of interest to herself. The thought of disappointing Logan by screwing this up was bad enough, but she really couldn't stand the idea of disappointing herself yet again.

Shoving her weird response to Shawn down deep inside of herself where she could forget it ever existed, Rhiannon did her best to focus on doing her job. Looking around the backyard, her ideas for the party exploded as she doubled—okay, tripled—the budget she'd had in mind. With a space like this, she practically had carte blanche as to what she could do. The challenge now would be to convince Shawn to let her run with her ideas—and his wallet.

The way the backyard was set up precluded one of her original ideas for a huge outdoor buffet—the seating was so sprawling it would be a huge trek to get back to the buffet table. But she could set up a bunch of small food stations, one in each of the alcoves... She began jotting a long list of notes as she wandered the grounds.

She stayed outside as long as she could, imagining one scenario after another. At one point Shawn murmured something about checking the pasta, but she didn't notice him leave. She was too engrossed in planning the event of the year.

Standing where she was, with the lawn spread out in front of her and the lake in the distance, she could

almost see the party. The lawn crowded with people in
jeans and sundresses as they threw beanbags into a big
clown's mouth. Or—excitement thrummed through her
as ideas flashed through her brain almost too quick for
her to process—they could base the games on famous
films that everyone knew and loved. Instead of pelt-
ing a clown with beanbags, it could be a giant shark's
mouth instead.

She had begun to scribble a note about Hollywood-
izing the games when a hand fell on her shoulder. Her
heart went into instant overdrive as her stomach tightened, painfully. Whirling around, hands clenched into
fists, it took her a second to realize Shawn was standing
there, staring at her like she'd lost her mind.

"Hey, I'm sorry." To his credit, he backed up instantly, both hands in the air. "I didn't mean to startle you, Rhiannon. You were off in your own little
world."

The fear that had slammed through her at his unex-
pected touch slowly dissipated, but she was left feeling
awkward and embarrassed. What kind of event coordinator whipped around, looking for blood, the second
her client tried to get her attention?

"Hey. You're going back into your head again—stop
it."

Shawn's voice was kind but firm, and this time when
he placed a hand on her she didn't flinch away. She just
stood there, looking at him, and wondering what she
could possibly say to make up for her idiotic behavior.
Besides the truth—and the truth was the last thing she
wanted to get into right now.

But Shawn was more of a gentleman than he looked.

Instead of pushing her for some explanation, he just waited for her to figure out what she wanted to say.

Determined to get her head back in the game, she said, "Sorry. I was deep in thought about your party. I've come up with a bunch of different ideas."

"Oh, yeah? Did you come up with any keepers?" He moved a little closer, surveyed the yard much as she had been doing before he'd interrupted her.

"Actually, I think I might have." Though the fear was gone, her heart was still beating a little too fast and his proximity wasn't making things any better. She took a few casual steps away from him.

"As I mentioned before, I'm not sure a huge, formal party is going to make the impression on these people that you're hoping for. If they're from Hollywood, they've probably been to a million of those. So what about if we do what we talked about the other day? We don't try to compete with what they're used to, but instead give them something else entirely? Maybe something more along the lines of a carnival?"

She spread her arms wide, gestured to all the different attractions he already had in place. "Your backyard is perfect for it. We can set up some big, brightly colored tents on the lawn, have people compete at games of chance for movie-themed prizes. You know, like carnival games—try to get three rings around a bottle, beanbag tosses, that kind of thing.

"And for food, we can set up different stations. Each station can be a takeoff of a famous Endeavor film. You know, like for *Desert Bandits* we can serve kabobs and other Middle Eastern finger foods. For *Broken Vines,* we can do a wine-tasting from some Central Texas vineyards with a bunch of gourmet breads and cheeses. *Kiss and Tell* can be the dessert tent, with a big chocolate fountain and sweets tables spread out all around it."

She paused, took a breath. Tried to read his face. She was so excited about the idea that she would be totally bummed if he rejected it. It was his party, of course, but everything inside her screamed that this would be perfect.

Plus, it was only the third big party she'd handled on her own since Logan had given her a job two years before—she'd handled a lot of smaller affairs, but until a few months ago the big ones had always gone through him. About six months ago he'd begun giving her bigger jobs—one of which was the party at which she'd met Shawn the previous Saturday—but she still worried about making mistakes.

About placing Logan in an awkward position, where he'd feel like he had to keep her because she was his friend instead of wanting to keep her because she did a kick-ass job.

About thinking too much like a journalist and not enough like an event coordinator. Old habits—and even some of her new ones—were turning out to be very hard to break.

"You know, I really like the idea."

"You do?" she whispered, thrilled at the confidence boost his answer gave her.

"Yeah. It's not the fancy thing I had originally planned on, but I can see where it could be a lot of fun. Plus, I know I'd enjoy a party like that a lot more than one where I had to sip champagne in a stuffy tuxedo."

"Excellent. I'll put some numbers together and work

up a minimum budget for this kind of thing. But before I do that, do you have a basic idea of how much you want to spend? I should have asked you the other day but—"

"But you were so dazzled by my charm and wit that you couldn't remember all the business details?" He grinned. "That's okay, I'm used to it."

She narrowed her eyes. "I was going to say it was because you'd been hassling me incessantly with your God's-gift-to-women persona and I just couldn't work it into the conversation."

"No, I don't think so." He tilted his head, as if actually considering the situation, but the expression on his face let her know he was only teasing. "I really do think you were just trying hard not to throw yourself at me. There's no reason to be embarrassed. Like I said, it happens to me all the time."

"I just bet it does." She started to roll her eyes, but thought better of it. Hadn't she just decided that she was going to keep things as businesslike as possible between them? Yet here she was, falling into a joking rhythm with him that was far easier to take part in than it should have been.

"Besides, I kind of like it."

"Like what?"

"The fact that you get all frazzled and nervous around me."

"Lissa didn't mention that you were delusional when she introduced us. I'll have to talk to her about that."

"Yeah, well, best friends and their wives don't know everything."

They stood there, grinning at each other, for long seconds. An owl hooted, followed by the long, lonely sound of a coyote howling. When she was at her condo in the city, she couldn't hear any of this. Couldn't hear much of anything besides people, despite the abundant greenbelt around her complex. Was it because she hadn't taken the time to listen in far too long? Because she couldn't stand the sound of silence—of her own thoughts—anymore and always had the stereo going?

A gust of wind blew past her and she shivered. Shawn stepped close, blocking the cold air from hitting her head-on. "Are you ready to go in?"

Was she? Rhiannon glanced around the yard she had such high hopes for and tried to recapture the excitement—the warmth—she'd been feeling just a few moments before. But the sad, solitary cries of the coyote echoed within her, reminding her of just how long she'd been alone. Just how long it had been since she'd been able to reach out for or accept any kind of closeness—physical or emotional.

Maybe it was time to change that. She was sick of being alone, sick of always being on the outside looking in. Shawn was nice—really nice—not to mention sexy as hell. Maybe if she took things slowly, if she got to know him while planning the party, she could see where things took them. In six weeks' time, when he was no longer a client, maybe she'd even be ready for a real date. One that ended in a real kiss and not just the glancing of his lips against her own.

It was an interesting idea, one she would have to consider for a while before she decided on it one way or another. But that was okay, because she had some time. Shawn wasn't going anywhere for a while, and neither was she.

"Hey, what's wrong?" He started to reach for her hand, then stopped himself. She could see from the look in his eyes that he was remembering her jumpiness when he'd touched her shoulder. Terrific—now he thought he was saddled with a total freak for a party planner. So much for him wanting to kiss her when this whole thing was over.

The thought jerked her out of her funk and Rhiannon forced herself to concentrate on the present. "Yeah, I'm fine. Just cold." She managed to work up the same carefree grin she'd used to fool her friends and family for months now.

"There's a cure for that, you know."

"Oh, yeah? What's that?" He was so close now that she had to tilt her head back to maintain eye contact. The air between them was suddenly charged, electric, and she wasn't sure how she felt about that. Part of her wanted to pull away, to shrink back inside the cocoon she'd built around herself and stay there. But another part of her, one that she barely recognized, wanted to stay right where she was. That part wanted to see what happened next.

But nothing happened next. Instead, he backed away with a relaxed expression that didn't quite reach his eyes. "A race to the house should cure your chills," he said. "On your mark. Get set. Go."

CHAPTER FIVE

SHAWN TOOK OFF BEFORE Rhiannon had registered his words, but kept his pace deliberately slow, conscious of her closing the distance between them. When she finally caught up to him, tossing him a cocky grin, he started to lay on the speed, but she looked so sexy with her hair streaming behind her and the navy dress molded to her curves that he let her pass just so he could enjoy the view of her running in front of him.

She hit the stairs a couple of seconds before he did, and shot him a look of mock-disgust over her shoulder. "Taking off without me like that was cheap."

He shrugged. "You won, didn't you?"

"You let me win—it's not the same thing."

"Do I sense a competitive spirit here?"

"What, does that surprise you?"

"A little bit. But that's okay—I like surprises." And Rhiannon was turning out to be the nicest surprise he'd had in a long time.

Tonight had only reinforced the idea he had had at the restaurant when he'd decided she was a contradiction, a puzzle. Rhiannon might look all prim and proper on the outside, but there was a lot more to her than met the eye. The fact that'd she'd taken up his challenge without thinking twice, the way she always had a zippy comeback for him, how she looked when she didn't know he was watching her—it all added up to a woman who ran a lot deeper than her surface made it seem.

He liked that about her, liked the fact that he had to work to figure her out and couldn't help wondering what she would be like if she ever really let go.

Stepping back, making sure not to crowd her, Shawn studied her for a moment and saw with satisfaction that the haunted look he'd noticed outside was gone from her eyes, and her pale cheeks were now flushed with color. He didn't know what had happened out there, what had turned her so suddenly skittish, but he'd known it was bad—even before she'd drifted away from him. "Come on, let's eat. I'm hungry."

"You're the one blocking the path to the kitchen."

"Excuse me." He moved to the side, gesturing for her to lead the way. Which she did with a flash of her dimple that told him, better than words, that she was trying to recover from what had happened outside.

Dinner was an almost relaxed affair, filled with talk of the party and a little bit of silly banter between them—initiated by him, of course. But Rhiannon kept up her end of the conversation, and he could tell by the gradual warming of her eyes that she was enjoying it almost as much as he was. He kept trying to make her laugh again, but her reserve had kicked in and the best he could get was an occasional quirk of her lips.

It wasn't enough for him, but he made do—especially as sitting across from Rhiannon was no hardship. She looked sexily disheveled—her hair tousled from the run, her cheeks pink, her dress just a little bit askew. It was a good look for her, one that was as far from the woman he'd first met at Robert and Lissa's party as she could get.

When it was her turn to talk, he got lost in the soft, melodic sound of her voice as she recounted some of her experiences as a party planner—including a few truly hilarious incidents that had him all but rolling on the floor with laughter. She complimented him on the food, again, and though it was one of his favorite meals, he barely paid any attention to it. He was too busy watching that crazy dimple of hers, cataloging the little laugh lines at the corners of her eyes, counting the freckles on her left cheek that formed a tiny star he wanted nothing more than to trace with his tongue.

Watching her, it occurred to him—not for the first time—that people would probably say she was too old for him. He didn't know her exact age, but his best guess put her at somewhere around thirty-six or thirty-seven, years older than his own twenty-nine. But it didn't matter to him, not when he couldn't remember the last time he'd enjoyed having dinner with a woman this much.

Besides, age had never been an issue to him when it came to women. While it was true that he'd never dated a woman more than one or two years older than him before, the idea didn't bother him as it would some of his friends. For him, it was all about the chemistry, about how he felt when he looked at a woman, talked to her, touched her. If she interested him, that was enough, and Rhiannon—with all of her stops and goes, all of her contradictions and complications—interested him more than any woman had in a long time.

Where else would he find a poised, sophisticated woman who was as interested in watching a slasher movie as she was in going to an art gallery? A woman who could discuss politics one minute and Willie Nelson and the city's Keep Austin Weird campaign the next? Who cared if she was twenty-seven or thirty-seven or even forty-seven as long as there was a spark between them? And while he still wasn't sure about Rhiannon's side, he knew that on his there was a hell of a lot more than a spark going on.

Now, if only he could get her interested in baseball, it'd be a match made in heaven.

When they were finished eating, she insisted on helping him clear the table before he ushered her into the family room he loved. The back wall was all windows and it had an incredible view of the lake—at the end of a long day of writing, he liked nothing more than sitting on his sofa and watching the sun set over Lake Travis.

"You know, we could set up a bar in the corner over there, along with a couple of food stations." Rhiannon stood in the middle of the room, turning in a slow circle as she examined every nook and cranny. As she did, he wondered how she could stand there, surrounded by such an incredible view—the lights were still on outside and his entire backyard had a soft, mellow glow—and think only of work. Especially when it was the farthest thing from his mind.

"Maybe a pasta station over here in this corner—very *Mafia Times*—and then in the center of the room, we could—"

"Do you ever think about anything but work?" he interrupted her, simply to see what she would do.

She didn't even break stride. "—have prizes for the games. Or at least a prize booth where they could trade

tickets in. Movie memorabilia, that kind of thing. I'm
not sure how much it would cost, but I think it could be
doable." She finally paused for a breath. "How much
are you thinking of budget wise? I started to ask you
when we were outside, but we got sidetracked."

"I don't know. What's a reasonable number for this
kind of party?"

She named a price that had his eyes widening and
his hand clutching at his wallet where it rested in the
back pocket of his jeans. Beer and chips weren't sounding so bad after all.

"For a casual party?" he asked incredulously. "How
much would the formal party have been?"

"Probably about the same," she admitted wryly. "If
that's more than you were wanting to spend, we can
tone things down a bit. There doesn't have to be—"

He cut her off before she could gain any more mo-
mentum and launch into another spiel, partly because
in the end he didn't care that much—after all, he had
the money—and partly because he could think of any
number of more interesting things to talk about with
her than the virtues of a party with a budget that just
might rival the national debt of a small country.

"Work up a budget for our next meeting, like
you were planning on, and we'll take it from there.
Okay?"

"Of course." She cleared her throat. "I should probably be going then."

"Why?"

"Why what?"

Her brow was furrowed in confusion and he wanted
nothing more then to step forward and smooth it out.
But, despite the fact that she'd relaxed some over dinner,

Rhiannon still had enough No Trespassing signs around her to stop a blind man in his tracks. "Why do you want to leave? You haven't even opened your present yet."

Her eyes narrowed. "You bought me a present?"

"I did." He crossed to the bar, pulled out the large, colorful bag he'd placed there earlier in the day, and held it out to her.

She didn't take it, didn't do anything but stare at the gift—and him—like they were cobras poised to strike. In return, he stayed right where he was, not saying anything, not moving, barely even breathing as he waited to see what she would do.

"Why would you do that? You barely know me."

"True, but I like what I do know of you. And as to why I bought the present—" He dangled it on a fingertip, watching as her eyes followed its back-and-forth motion as if hypnotized. "I saw it at the store today and it made me think of you. Besides, your education is sorely lacking in some areas and I thought this could even it out a little."

"Sorely lacking?" From the look on her face, he could tell she wasn't sure whether she should be insulted or not. Which was fine with Shawn, as the confusion—and mild insult—propelled her across the room to him.

"What's in the bag?" she demanded, when she was only a few steps away.

He extended his arm so that she only had to come a couple feet closer to look inside it. "Why don't you look inside and find out?"

She didn't move for the longest time, and neither did he, though the waiting was killing him. He loved to give presents, loved to see how the woman in his life

reacted when she got them, but he'd never had anyone
react to a gift from him quite like Rhiannon was. Her
suspicion made him a little sad—not to mention angry
at the bastard who had hurt her enough that a simple
foil bag could have her gnawing on her lip until she
was close to drawing blood.

"Whatever it is, it better be good," she said finally,
reaching for the bag with a touch of defiance. Her fingers rubbed against his and a little shock of electricity
crackled through him, between them, as he felt her skin
brush his. Her eyes darkened to a deep, molten chocolate and he waited for her to pull away. But she didn't.
Instead, she let her fingers linger for a few seconds, as
if—in that moment—she was as curious about the feel
of him as he was about her.

And then she was pulling away, the connection between them severed, though heat lingered in the air
between them. Shawn stared at her, wondering what
she was thinking. What she was feeling. Whatever it
was, she had a poker face and projected nothing but
a calm serenity he knew she couldn't be feeling, not
while the gift bag she now held was rustling with each
tremor of her fingertips.

After a minute, she broke eye contact and started
rummaging through the bag, pulling out the tissue paper
he'd crumpled up and shoved in the top a few hours
before. After laying it neatly on the bar, she finally
reached in and pulled out his present. For a second,
she didn't react at all, just stared at his gift in silence.
And then she started to laugh—not a small, tinkling
giggle like he'd heard before but a warm, full-bodied
laugh that filled up the entire room around them.

He felt himself grow hard at the sound, and at the

sight of her so free and uninhibited. So unselfcon-
scious. He watched her, fascinated by the transforma-
tion, and wondered—which was the real Rhiannon?
This woman with the big laugh and dancing eyes, or
the sedate woman who always dressed in neutrals and
rarely made a move she hadn't thought out?

The contradictions were driving him insane, the
edges of the puzzle refusing to fit together in his mind
no matter how hard he tried to find the right angle.
There were too many missing pieces, too many stories
left unsaid. Tonight he'd gotten one of those pieces.
He'd have to wait and see what other ones showed up
in the next few days and weeks.

"You bought me slasher movies?" she asked, a little
incredulously.

"Not just any slasher movies. I will have you know
that you are holding the Saturday Night Cinema Special
in your hot little hands—the trifecta of slasher movies,
The greatest slasher movies of all time, bar none."

"According to you."

"According to anyone who has taste. I'm telling you,
if you're as big a fan of the genre as you say you are,
then it is an absolute travesty that you haven't seen
those movies."

"A travesty you just had to remedy?"

"Well, obviously. And look—" He pointed at the
large cardboard tub the movies had been resting in.
"I even got you popcorn and an extra-large chocolate
bar."

"I'm more of a gummy-worm girl myself."

"Who isn't? But the store was out of gummy worms,
so I had to improvise. Next time, I'll go with the gummy
eyeballs."

"There's going to be a next time?"

He sighed with exaggerated patience, loving the spark that came to her eyes. "Of course there will be. I have an entire wall of horror films and I won't rest until you've seen them all."

"That's quite a sacrifice you're making there."

"It'll be tough, but someone's got to do it."

"I just bet." Rhiannon leaned back against the bar, more relaxed than he had ever seen her. It made his blood boil and his erection throb and he was seized by a nearly overwhelming urge to kiss her. But he hadn't come this far to blow it when he was so close to the prize.

For Rhiannon was a double-edged sword, one that required a very careful balancing act. Normally that would be enough to make him run in the other direction—after Cynthia had killed herself, he'd made a point of sliding through life with a wink and a smile, steering clear of any major complications or entanglements.

But this was different, this energy that pulsed between Rhiannon and him whenever they got too close. It was sweet yet exciting, sexy yet comfortable—as much a mystery and a contradiction as Rhiannon was herself. Even knowing that she was a risk—that he might very well end up on his ass six weeks from now, watching as she zoomed off into her own sunset—couldn't keep him from wanting her.

"So, I suppose you want to watch these movies with me?"

"Well, since you asked so nicely..."

"I appreciate the gift—I really do. It was incredibly thoughtful. But..." She paused and he waited for the brush-off he could tell was coming. It upset him, because he knew, deep down, that they could be good together. But she had to know it, too, or at least suspect it. Otherwise, it didn't do him any good to stand around mooning over her.

"You know it can only be business between us, Shawn."

And there it was, the line he'd been waiting for. "Why?"

"Because you're a client, one whose event is going to bring in big word of mouth for my firm. I can't afford to get tangled up with you."

"Okay." He shrugged. "You're fired, then. Problem solved."

Her eyes widened. "The problem is definitely not solved. I can't afford to let you fire me. My boss would kill me."

"Well, then, what do you suggest we do? Because I'm not willing to just forget being with you, talking to you, simply because I hired your firm to do my party."

"It's a conflict of—"

"Don't give me that tired old line about conflicts of interest." He moved closer to her, crowded her just a little bit even as he told himself it was the wrong move.

But he couldn't help it. He wanted to be near her, wanted to feel the silky soft brush of her skin against his again. Wanted to smell her sweet honeysuckle scent. He didn't touch her—he still had enough control not to do that—but he couldn't make himself take that step back, no matter how much he knew he should.

"Because if you feed me that line, it means one of

two things. Either you're not interested in me and you're looking for a convenient excuse to step back gracefully, or you are interested and I should just eliminate the conflict so that we can move forward." He took a deep breath, inhaled her into his lungs. "So which one is it, Rhiannon? Do you want to go on a third date with me or don't you?"

"This isn't a date," she protested, but it was weak and he could tell she knew it.

"Yeah, well, it sure as hell isn't a business dinner." He glanced at the clock. "At least, not exclusively a business dinner."

"It was supposed to be." Her voice sounded desperate, and her big coffee-brown eyes pleaded with him to let the subject drop.

He didn't want to. He wanted to follow the thing through, to figure out where they stood once and for all. But she was looking a little panicked and he couldn't ignore that—not when he'd made certain, his entire life, never to deliberately make a woman uncomfortable.

"All right, then." He forced himself to ease back, but it was a lot harder than it should have been. "Business, it is. For now."

He nodded to the gift bag still in her hands. "Enjoy the movies. Start with the top one—it's the best."

Tension throbbed between them, though he did his best to alleviate it by walking around the bar and putting the width of the thing between them. He poured himself a whiskey, then asked, "Do you want anything?"

"No. I'm driving."

"Right. Of course you are."

"Don't be mad, Shawn."

"I'm not mad. I don't play that game. I'm just… disappointed."

"Why?" she asked, and he could tell she was talking about a lot more than the fact that she'd turned him down. The vulnerable look in her eyes said she was asking why he was interested in her to begin with.

"Don't you feel this thing between us, Rhiannon? You have to, right? I can't be in this alone, not when it feels so incredibly right to be near you. To listen to you talk. To try to make you smile, which isn't very easy, by the way. To watch you—"

She cut him off by leaning across the bar and pressing her lips against his own

It was over almost before it began, as Rhiannon broke the kiss off and backed away.

He followed her, forcing himself to walk around the bar instead of jumping over it as his suddenly rampaging libido had him contemplating.

"I think," she said unsteadily, "that we should both concentrate on making this party successful."

"I'm a great multitasker. I can concentrate on more than one thing at once." The tension between them stretched taut as a fishing line and he took another step closer to her. He wanted to taste her, wanted to feel her lips against his one more time before she walked away.

Rhiannon swallowed convulsively and her hand came up to rest on his chest. At first he thought she meant to push him away, and he started to back up, ruthlessly squelching the surge of disappointment that swept through him.

But then her fingers twisted in his shirt, clung. And he knew he had her—even if it was just for this moment.

"Let me touch you, Rhiannon." He murmured the request softly, not wanting to spook her. Still, if he didn't kiss her soon—really kiss her—he was afraid he might embarrass himself for the first time since he was a teenager.

"You are touching me." Her voice was even softer than his.

"Actually, you're touching me." He brought his head lower, until only a breath separated them. "Let me kiss you."

Her eyes widened, the pupils dilating against the dark brown of her irises, and he felt her fear   and her arousal—in every cell in his body. "I want—"

"I won't hurt you. I promise." He stroked her cheek soothingly. "I just want to know what you feel like. What you taste like."

She was trembling, from fear or desire he didn't know. The idea that he had inadvertently frightened her upset him, and he started to back away, but once again, at the last possible second, she leaned forward and closed the distance between them. Her mouth brushed against his—once, twice—as tentative as a hummingbird. As sweet as a flower petal.

He wanted to let her control the kiss the first time, to let her take him instead of the other way around. But as her lips parted in a warm, sweet sigh, he lost everything but the driving need to taste her.

Sliding his hands around to the back of Rhiannon's head, he tangled his fingers in her hair, then brought her in closer until his lips were a steady pressure on hers.

His tongue stroked across her mouth, exploring the funny little indention in the center of her upper lip, the plump fullness of her bottom lip.

Toying with the upturned corner of her mouth.

Licking over the scar that ran to the right of her dimple.

She tasted delicious, exotic, like roses and pomegranates and the darkest, richest honey. He wanted to savor her like the finest cognac, to take her slowly and enjoy every nuance of her heady flavor.

He also wanted to gobble her up like the tastiest of treats, to rush to the end zone and then start all over again at the zero yard line.

In the end, he did a little of both. He played with her lower lip, pulled it between his teeth and nipped gently. She moaned and the fingers that were still tangled in his shirt dug deeper as she returned his exploration with her own.

It was his turn to groan as need all but overwhelmed him. His hands swept down her back, enveloped her, pulled her in closer. Her mouth opened on a sigh and he took her breath deep inside of him, then slipped inside her to explore her warmth.

He licked over the top of her mouth, stroked his tongue along her cheek and the inside of her upper lip. He'd just begun to wonder how Rhiannon felt about making love against the wall when she wrenched herself away from him.

She stood there for long seconds, breathing hard. Her lips were swollen, her hands curled into fists. And her eyes—her eyes were more turbulent than he had ever seen them. And more empty.

"Rhiannon." He reached for her, but she was already turning across the family room, through the foyer, out the front door to her waiting car. He let her go, because he wanted—too badly—to stop her.

CHAPTER SIX

WHAT HAD SHE DONE? Rhiannon wondered as she sped away from Shawn's house. What had she been thinking, kissing him like that? Letting him kiss her like that? Her lips still burned from where he'd licked and sucked at them.

She didn't want this. Not now, maybe not ever. And certainly not with a man she barely knew.

After she'd been raped by a source she had considered completely trustworthy, her husband had had a hard time understanding her moods and her phobias. He'd had an even harder time dealing with her fear of being touched by a man, any man—even her husband. He had tried to get through to her, had tried to reach her behind the solid wall of ice she had erected between herself and the rest of the world. But finally Richard had given up, walked away. Divorced her and moved on in a way she hadn't been able to.

And he had always been a stand-up guy—still was one, if she was completely honest about it. Smart, responsible, loving, he'd been a good husband, all the way until the divorce.

The problem had been within her. Her inability to get beyond the attack, to find her way through the fear and depression and hopelessness to connect with him, had eventually been too much for him to take. If one of

the most dependable men she'd ever known could get
fed up enough with her to walk away after fifteen years
of marriage, it was crazy to think that Shawn—with
his crooked smile and life's-a-party attitude—would
stick around long enough to even skim the surface of
her issues.

Besides, even if he did stick around, it wasn't like
she could handle his interest, not when some days
she still felt like she could fall apart at the slightest
provocation.

So, what the hell had she been thinking? Had she
really thought she was healed enough to kiss him?

Had she really thought attraction would be enough,
when her very handsome, attractive husband hadn't
been able to reach her, no matter what he'd tried?

When the only way she could get through the day
was by controlling herself and every element in her
life?

She had to have been insane. There was no other
explanation for it. She'd known that he was interested
when she went over there, had certainly known he
wanted to pursue something when she'd realized he'd
made her dinner…and bought her a present. And still,
she hadn't walked away.

No, not her. She'd been stupid enough to think that
maybe, just maybe, she could do this thing. It didn't
have to be serious, didn't have to be a big deal. As she'd
looked at the red bag dangling from his fingertips, she'd
decided that maybe it could be okay. Maybe she could
just hang out with a handsome, exciting man who made
her laugh.

Instead, she'd kissed him and then totally freaked

out, running out of the house like the hounds of hell were after her. It was too humiliating for words.

And if it wasn't bad enough that she had just completely embarrassed herself, it wasn't like she could go home and hide away in shame until she found a way to move past the whole, terrible episode. No, she had to see him again in a few days, had to talk to him. Had to go over party plans with him.

How the hell was she supposed to do that?

Stopping at a red light, Rhiannon rested her head on the steering wheel and counted slowly to ten as she reminded herself that this was not the end of the world. She'd gotten through a lot worse than this. She might not be whole, but she was still standing. That had to count for something.

And as for Shawn, from here on out, she would deal with him as she would any other client. She would email him about the party, make sure to keep their phone conversations strictly professional, and in no way encourage him ever again.

Ever. Again. She wasn't ready to do this male-female thing and she was done trying. Attraction or not, she was taking herself firmly out of the game Shawn had pieced together for them.

It was better that way. She'd spent long enough on an emotional roller coaster. It was time to get off the ride.

RHIANNON WAS DRIVING him crazy. Insane. Completely bonkers with her refusal to pick up the phone when he called or to return his messages. It had been more than a week since she'd yanked herself from his arms and gone running out of his house like the place was on fire and he hadn't been able to get her to say one word to him. Not one word.

Oh, she'd been in touch with him. She'd emailed him the proposed budget, faxed him a few ideas for the menu that she wanted him to look over, even texted him with a few questions that she needed clarified. But not once had she actually spoken to him, no matter how many messages he'd left her.

It was enough to make a perfectly sane man lose his mind. It was more than enough to drive that same man to do an insane amount of grueling exercise.

Shawn pounded up the last hill that separated him from his house, his steps steady, his breathing easy despite the five miles he had just put in running up and down the hills that surrounded Lake Travis.

Maybe he'd stand a chance in that marathon Robert had signed him up for, after all. It was in four weeks, and like nearly everything else in his life that he didn't like to do, his training schedule had been haphazard at best. At least until Rhiannon had messed with his mind—and his libido.

But then, why would he want to train seriously for the stupid marathon anyway? He didn't know why he was running the thing—except for the fact that Robert had issued the challenge. Of course, he'd only done so because he wanted someone to run with him, and he'd known that the one thing Shawn had trouble passing up was a challenge.

That was one of the many reasons he was so interested in Rhiannon—she was a hell of a challenge. Extremely difficult to get a handle on and more work than any woman had ever been for him, bar none.

But with Rhiannon, he didn't mind the work. He

actually kind of liked it, he acknowledged as he ran steadily toward his house, despite the fact that she sent out so many mixed signals that he barely knew whether he was coming or going with her. And he was trying to respect the fact that she didn't want to go out with him. After the first message he'd left, the others had been strictly professional, focusing on the party and all the questions she needed answered.

At the same time, he couldn't help remembering the way she'd kissed him—with a passion so hot it had nearly burned him. He wanted to feel that heat again, wanted to feel *her* again. Giving her time to work things out in her own head was driving him nuts, especially since he was afraid she'd already done so— just not in his favor.

He wanted to get to know her, wanted to find out what was underneath that cool, collected exterior. Maybe that's all she was—calm and competent, through and through. But that kiss last week had been anything but calm. Anything but collected. He'd dreamed about it the past several nights—had dreamed about her— and had woken up each morning hard and aching and desperate for her.

It was crazy, he thought again as he slammed into his house and headed straight for the shower. Crazy how she'd gotten under his skin. Even crazier how he couldn't get her back out again.

So what was he supposed to do? he wondered, as he stepped under the hot water and let it beat out the tension in his shoulders. Was he supposed to chase after her like a puppy, hoping for a little of her time? Or should he move on, forget all about the fact that she made his mouth dry and his hands shake? It wasn't like he needed that kind of complication right now, anyway. Wasn't like he wanted to fall for her. Walking away was definitely the smarter move.

Yet smarter didn't always equal best, and he couldn't help wondering if this was one of those times. Closing his eyes, he shampooed his hair before letting the warm water sluice the suds away. That was the problem— from the minute he'd seen her at Robert's party, he hadn't been thinking clearly, hadn't been on his game. And while he normally liked to just take things as they came—to fly by the seat of his pants—everything inside of him told him that wasn't going to work with Rhiannon.

For her, he needed a very detailed plan, much like the mock-ups he did for his novels before he actually started the artwork. He needed to lay down his battle strategy according to the rules she'd provided, sketchy as they were. Because if he'd figured out anything at all while he'd been running his ass off this week, it was that he wasn't ready to see the last of her. Not even close.

Turning the water off, he stepped out of the shower. Grabbing a towel on the fly, he headed straight for the phone on his nightstand, with only one thought in his mind.

Game on.

By the time he was done, Rhiannon wouldn't even know what had hit her.

CHAPTER SEVEN

"Hey, have you been holding out on me?"

Rhiannon looked up from the plans she'd been finalizing for a sixtieth wedding anniversary to find Logan leaning against her doorway, an inquisitive look on his too-handsome face.

"Of course I have—in every way possible." She grinned. "So you're going to have to be a little more specific if you want me to know what you're talking about."

Logan raised one sardonic eyebrow, then reached behind him for a huge arrangement of tulips in a beautiful, crystal vase. "I was referring to these."

"Oh, wow! They're gorgeous."

"They are." He walked over and set them on her desk. "So, I ask again, are you holding out on me?"

"What do you mean?" She stared, puzzled, at the flowers. "Why are you bringing those in here?"

"Because they're for you, Ding Dong."

"For me?" She was dumbfounded as she stared at the gorgeous array of tulips. There were red ones and white ones, hot pinks, yellows, purples and oranges. A regular cacophony of colors that shouldn't have gone together but did, beautifully.

"Well, they certainly aren't for me."

It had been so long since someone had sent her

flowers, and such exquisite ones at that. Sure, Richard had given her flowers at the beginning of their relationship, but nothing in the past few years of their marriage, as they'd settled into a rut and he'd been more concerned with saving money than making her smile. And never had he sent her anything like these.

These flowers looked like a party in a vase. Cheerful, whimsical, elegant—exactly how she'd always wanted to see herself but had never been able to.

Rhiannon reached tentatively for the card, unsure she wanted to read it. There was only one man she could imagine sending her flowers like this. Only one man who seemed to understand that there was more to her than the mask she wore, and she'd spent the past eight days dodging his phone calls.

In the end, she couldn't resist. Ripping open the envelope, she pulled out the small white card and braced herself for whatever it might say.

Because I don't know your favorite color—yet. Enjoy, Shawn.

A silly smile passed across her face, one she was wont to stop, even knowing that Logan was studying her with the concentration of a cat on the trail of a very plump mouse. She leaned forward, burying her face in the tender blooms and breathed in their subtle, sophisticated scent.

"So, are you going to spill the beans or what? Sandy will launch a full investigation when I get home and I need to have something to tell her."

"It's no big deal—just a thank-you from a client."

Logan snorted. "I've seen client thank-yous before, and very rarely do they encompass a hundred dollars worth of sexy, elegant flowers."

"Well, that's all it is."

"Okay." He held up his hands, as if surrendering as he settled into the chair on the other side of her desk. "So which client is this?"

Rhiannon tucked the card into her pants pocket, and pretended to be looking over the budget for the Waters' anniversary party. The fact that she couldn't see the numbers—couldn't see anything but Shawn's smiling face—was no one's business but her own.

"Shawn Emerson." She kept her voice casual.

"Really? He's more interested than you originally thought, hmm?"

"It's not like that," Rhiannon protested, a familiar sense of panic starting to well up inside of her. It had been nearly a year since she'd had a panic attack— although the whole debacle at Shawn's the previous Saturday had come close—but she recognized the beginnings of one now in her too-fast heartbeat and the fine trembling that seemed to be working its way through her body.

She pushed away from her desk, dropped her head to her knees and tried to breathe.

Why is this happening now? she wondered frantically. *Why am I losing it today when it's been so long since I've had one of these things?*

She was stupid, a total idiot. How could she expect to ever actually date Shawn when the mere act of getting flowers from him sent her into a full-blown panic?

She could tell herself she was ready to date all she wanted, but coping with a physical relationship with a man—any man, even the very attractive Shawn Emerson—was too much for her to handle.

She was aware of Logan's footsteps crossing the

room, aware of her office door closing, though she knew he hadn't left. Extremely conscious of Logan watching, Rhiannon tried to sit up, to look normal, but the room was spinning and it was all she could do to force her lungs to accept air. Pretending that she was fine was completely beyond her.

"Oh, sweetie, it's okay." Logan came around the desk and crouched down beside her. He ran a hand over her hair, down her neck to her back, where he rubbed in soothing circles.

Suddenly it was all too much—the idea of stepping outside the safe world she'd made for herself these past few years, of actually moving on with her life—and she launched herself at her oldest, dearest friend.

Logan caught her, his arms coming around her as she buried her face in his neck and started to sob. He settled on the floor, pulled her onto his lap and started to rock, back and forth, as he made soothing sounds.

She knew she should stop, knew she should be embarrassed—she was acting like a complete basket case when she'd promised herself that she wouldn't do that anymore. But she couldn't stop. Neither the tears nor the panic nor the pain that was racing through her like a runaway semi. So instead, she melted into Logan and let herself pretend, for a little while anyway, that she was safe.

She didn't know how long they sat there, Logan comforting her as she fell apart, but eventually the panic receded and her sobs quieted. She started to pull away, but he held her to him, refusing to let her go yet.

"I made a mess of your sweater."

"Screw my sweater." But he shifted her weight a

little, reached up and pulled some tissues out of the box she had resting on her desk.

She wiped her eyes, blew her nose. Did everything she could not to look at him. Finally, when she could avoid it no longer, she murmured, "I'm sorry. I promised myself I wouldn't do this anymore."

"Wouldn't do what?" he asked, still rubbing her back in soothing circles.

"Fall apart like this. I feel like such a jerk."

"You're not a jerk—an idiot, maybe."

"Hey!" She leaned back, punched him in the shoulder.

"And she's back." Logan climbed to his feet, settling her in her desk chair as he did. "Nobody expects you to stay in control all the time, you know. Nobody but you, that is."

"It's been almost three years—"

"So what? Is there some kind of timeline for getting over something like this that I'm not aware of?"

"You can say it, you know. I won't break if you say the word."

"No, but I might." He settled, grim-faced, onto the side of her desk. "Rhiannon, have you ever thought that maybe you should cut yourself some slack?"

"I have! I've done nothing but make excuses for my behavior for two and a half years, done nothing but let you and Matt and the rest of my family make those same excuses."

"That is such bullshit. Such self-pitying bullshit that I can't even believe it came out of your mouth."

Rhiannon felt her mouth literally fall open as her eyes jerked to Logan's. "What did you say?"

"You've been healing, Rhiannon. Getting a little bit

better with every month and year that passes. Pretending differently just makes you look weak—something we both know that you aren't."

"I just had a panic attack on my office floor because some guy sent me flowers. I wouldn't exactly call that strong. Or healthy."

"Why not?"

"What?"

He shrugged. "You've spent more than two and a half years hiding from men, denying your own sexuality."

She started to protest, but he stopped her with a raised hand. "And that's perfectly understandable. What happened to you—" His voice shook with repressed anger, but he took a breath. Shoved it back. "What happened to you was terrible. Awful. And then what Richard did on top of it? Is it any wonder that the idea of a man seeing you as desirable stresses you out?"

"I can't do this, Logan. I thought I could, I thought I was ready, but I just can't."

"No one says you have to. Thank Emerson for the flowers and tell him you aren't interested in him that way."

She didn't answer right away and Logan's gaze turned speculative. "But you can't do that, either, can you? Because you are interested in him."

"No."

"Yes. We've been friends for twenty-four years, Rhiannon. Do you really think you can lie to me? You're doing that pencil trick again."

"I am not!" But damn it, she was. Shoving out of her chair, she paced from one end of the small room to the other, then turned and worked her way back. Again and again as she tried to get her thoughts together, to formulate what she wanted to say.

"You keep turning yourself around like that and you're going to make both of us dizzy."

She pinned him with an annoyed stare. "You sound like my therapist."

"I'm just trying to figure out what you're really upset about—that you don't want to go out with Emerson or that you do?"

"I don't know, I don't know, I don't know!" She leaned against the wall, banged her head into it a couple of times. "He's smart, funny, good-looking—and years too young for me. I swear, I could practically be his mother. Not to mention the fact that he's completely ridiculous, all about fun, all the time."

"In other words, the complete opposite of the guys you used to be attracted to."

"Exactly. Which makes me wonder why I'm interested in him. *If* I'm even interested in him, or if I'm just using him to hide from the kind of men I really like. The kind I could build a real relationship with."

"First of all, you're thirty-nine—nowhere near old enough to be this guy's mother. And secondly, you're not the same person you were before. Maybe Emerson is exactly the kind of guy you need right now. Every relationship doesn't have to go somewhere, you know."

"Says the man who's been married to his high school sweetheart for almost twenty years now."

"Hey, just because I got lucky doesn't mean I don't know how the world works." He paused, seemed to consider his words. "Do you think Emerson is serious about you?"

"No. Of course not—he isn't serious about anything."

"So what's wrong with going on a date with him? It's not a lifelong commitment, just an agreement to spend a couple of hours together. If you like him, fine. If you don't, no harm, no foul."

Wasn't that exactly what she had told herself before Shawn had kissed her? That she could just have fun with him, see how things went? Of course, that was before she'd run away like an idiot and then freaked out so badly her best friend had had to talk her down off a ledge. "You know, not everything in life can be settled by a baseball metaphor."

"Maybe not. But the world would be a better place if it could be."

She scrubbed her hands over his eyes. "He's a client, Logan! The whole thing is inappropriate anyway."

"He's probably a one-time client—you said fancy, planned events weren't his thing. Besides, if neither of you is planning on pledging your undying love for the other, I don't see the problem. And I'm the boss—if I say there's no problem, there's no problem."

"Oh, really? Since when did this become a dictatorship?"

"Since you needed it to be. Now, get off your butt and call him."

Before she could come up with any more arguments, there was a frantic knock on the door. "Come in," Logan called, and the receptionist, Terri, shoved the door open, sticking her head into the room.

"There's a guy here to see you," she hissed.

"To see me?" Logan asked with a wink toward Rhiannon.

"No! To see *her*. And can I just say, he is hot. I mean, totally *f-i-n-e, fine*. With a capital *F*." Terri paused for breath and seemed to take in Rhiannon's disheveled, tear-stained appearance for the first time. "But I've got to say, you don't look so good. Maybe I should tell him you're busy?"

Rhiannon wanted to jump on the lifeline and have Terri do just that. She wasn't ready to face Shawn. Wasn't ready to face herself. But a quick glance at Logan told her what she already knew—if she didn't do this now, she very likely never would. And she just wasn't willing to give up on herself—to give up on living—quite that easily. She'd fought too hard to heal to just give it all up at the first sign of adversity.

"No, that's okay." She dug down deep, tried desperately to find a little of the courage she hadn't already used up. "Tell him I'm finishing up a call but that I'll be out in a minute."

As Terri left to convey her message, Rhiannon glanced down at the gray carpet that covered her office floor, wondering why it felt like the whole world had just crumbled beneath her feet.

CHAPTER EIGHT

"HEY." SHAWN SMILED at Rhiannon as she made her way through her office's fancy lobby toward him. It was his first time at Parties by L.K. and he was astonished at how upscale the place was. There must be a lot more money in event planning in Austin than he had ever imagined.

As Rhiannon passed beneath the high windows that lined two walls of the lobby, light reflected off the deep auburn of her hair, making him realize that it really wasn't red at all. Or at least, not exclusively red. There were strands of gold and burgundy and silver—and all the colors in between. It suited her, better than plain red ever could.

"Hey yourself." Her answering smile was more tentative than his had been and as he got his first good look at her face, he realized that she was upset. Even worse, she had been crying.

"Is this a bad time?" he asked warily. He didn't like it when women cried, didn't have the first idea of how to deal with it when they started leaking—which was why he'd always made it a firm policy to be out the door long before the tears came. He hadn't followed that policy when he'd lived with Cynthia and in the end, she'd nearly destroyed him along with herself.

As he looked at the tearstains Rhiannon hadn't been

able to hide, he waited for the old, familiar urge to run to kick in. But it didn't come. Its absence was as concerning as Rhiannon's tears and had him wondering—for the first time—if he was in deeper here than he'd ever thought.

But that was ridiculous. No matter what he said when he teased her, Rhiannon and he had never even had a proper date. How deep could he possibly be into this thing? Besides, his lack of desire to flee probably came from the fact that he was coming in on the other end of the deal—Rhiannon's eyes were red and a little puffy, her skin still a little blotchy despite the makeup she'd obviously just reapplied, but she was obviously done with the tears.

And then it was too late for a graceful exit anyway, as she murmured, "Thank you for the flowers. They're beautiful."

"They reminded me of you." As soon as the words were out of his mouth, he wanted to cut off his tongue. How corny could he get? Usually he was a lot smoother than this, but something about her was getting him too worked up to think clearly.

Besides, she didn't seem to think the line was all that corny. Her cheeks flushed a delicate rose and her eyes turned to that deep chocolate color he was learning to watch for—the one that told him she was lowering her guard.

"I think that's the nicest thing anyone has said to me in a long time."

"That tulips made them think of you?"

"Yes."

He shook his head, reached for her hand. "Obviously, you've been hanging out with the wrong crowd.

But that's okay, I'm here now." He started pulling her toward the door.

"Hey, what are you doing?"

"Taking you out of here. I've got some ideas for our third date and want to see what you think."

"I can't just leave." She glanced frantically at the watch on her wrist. "It's not even six o'clock yet. I still have some things to take care of—"

"Is one day really going to hurt you?"

"Probably not, but my desk is a mess and I haven't finished confirming flower orders for a party next week."

He paused, sighed. "If I give you a few minutes to finish things up, will that make it easier for you to leave with me?"

She nodded, nerves and excitement building inside of her. "Yes."

"So go, do what you need to do. I'll just sit right here and wait for you."

Rhiannon went back to her office with every intention of completing the things she'd told Shawn she needed to do. Instead, all she did was stand there staring at the wild assortment of tulips he'd sent her. Finally, she gave up, grabbed her coat and headed back to the front of the building.

"That was fast," Shawn said, as he popped up from where he'd been sitting, flipping through a magazine.

"I decided the work could wait."

"That's the spirit! Come on, let's go."

Shawn laughed at the look of complete befuddlement on Rhiannon's face as he swept her out into the bustling streets of downtown Austin. "Come on, slowpoke. We've got too much to do and not enough time to do it!"

"Too much to do?" she echoed, sounding like the parrot he'd gotten as a present for his twelfth birthday.

"Definitely."

"I thought this was supposed to be a date."

"It is."

"Don't dates generally involve food of some kind? Conversation?" she asked as they hustled over the Congress Avenue Bridge and passed a number of large hotels. "I know it's been a while since I've done this, but I do remember that being the generally accepted method of dating."

So it *had* been a while since she'd dated. He filed the information away, reminding himself that he needed to go slowly with her—which he would do, *after* he got her to their destination.

"We're almost there."

"Almost where?" she asked.

"You'll see."

"Are you always so secretive?"

"I don't know. Maybe. Sometimes." He shrugged. "Yeah, I guess I am. Does it bother you?"

"Not when you're obviously so definitive about it."

"That's me, Mr. Decisive."

"I can see that."

Grabbing her hand, he made a quick right onto the walking trails that surrounded Town Lake.

"Are we going down to the water?"

He shot her an amused look. "I bet you drove your mother crazy as a child. You don't do surprises very well, do you?"

She threw back her head and laughed, and his heart nearly stopped. This wasn't the low, tinkling laugh that she pulled out in socially appropriate situations, but the one he'd heard the night he'd given her the movies, a real laugh, one that lit her up from the inside and transformed her from beautiful to unbelievably stunning.

"I hate surprises. When I was a kid, I was always the one shaking the presents under the Christmas tree, trying to figure out what was in the boxes."

"Really? I wouldn't have guessed that about you."

"Oh, I was terrible. I still am, actually. My husband—" Her voice trailed off awkwardly and he nearly had a heart attack.

"You were married?" He used the past tense deliberately, telling himself that she would never have kissed him if she had a man waiting for her at home.

"Yes. For almost fifteen years. We divorced two years ago."

He wasn't sure how he felt about that, wasn't sure what to say. For the first time since they'd met, their age difference yawned between them. Seventeen years ago he'd been in seventh grade, playing baseball and discovering girls while she'd been getting married. She could have been young when she married, right out of high school, but somehow he didn't think so. Rhiannon didn't seem the type to rush into anything, let alone marriage.

He glanced at her and realized she was watching him carefully, almost as if she could see the thoughts running through his head. Their pace had slowed considerably and as he glanced at the darkening sky, he realized they were going to have to book it if they were going to make it on time.

"Come on, they're going to leave without us."

He could see the lightbulb come on. "We're going on a bat cruise?" she asked, glancing at the Congress Street Bridge, where thousands upon thousands of bats congregated during the spring and summer.

"That's the plan—but the boat leaves thirty minutes before sunset."

"Let's go, then." This time she grabbed his hand and they took off at a near run. "Do you know, except for college, I've lived in Austin my whole life and I've never been on one of these?"

"Really? I come a couple times each year. It's great."

"I bet. I've always wanted to come, I just never got around to it."

"All work and no play…"

"Yeah, yeah, yeah. I've heard it all before."

They finally got to the boat—with about two minutes to spare. Shawn paid for the tickets, then led her onto the old-fashioned paddleboat. Rhiannon shivered as they found a couple of seats near the front railing and he slipped an arm around her shoulders.

Her body tensed up and the look she gave him was both startled and wary. For a minute, he was sure she was going to pull away, but then—out of nowhere—she relaxed against him, her body melding to his.

It felt surprisingly good to hold her like this. No expectations, no plans, nothing but the feel of her soft curves against his chest.

They sat that way for a long time as the boat began its cruise around the lake. As they slowly made their way through the water, he watched the people running on the paths near the lake. Smiled at the families picnicking under the bridge as they waited for the bats to emerge. Enjoyed the feel of the cool air on his face.

And wondered, incessantly, what was going on in Rhiannon's head.

He had just opened his mouth to break the silence between them, when Rhiannon said, "I'll be forty in a few weeks."

"What?" he asked, not sure he had heard her correctly. Her voice had been even lower than usual.

"I know you were thinking about it, up there on the path, because I was thinking about your age, too. I'm thirty-nine."

Knowing it was his turn to ante up, he said, "I turned twenty-nine last month."

She nodded. "I figured you were close to thirty."

Now he was the one to flush. "I didn't have a clue you were almost forty."

"No?" She raised an eyebrow in that way that drove him absolutely crazy. "How old did you think I was?"

"I don't know. Thirty-four. Thirty-five, maybe."

"Flatterer." She turned to gaze out at the water. He waited for her to turn back to him, waited for her to say something for what seemed like forever. Just as he gave up and was about to speak himself, she whispered, "I totally understand if you want to change your mind—"

"It doesn't matter."

She did turn to him then. "Of course it matters. Eleven years—"

"Is no big deal. We're both grown-ups. And really, it doesn't matter to me." He paused. "Unless it matters to you."

"If I admit that it does matter, that it *does* bother me, does that make me shallow?"

"No. It makes you honest. But really, does it bother you that much?" He held his breath as he waited for her answer.

"It kind of does. I mean, I used to make fun of men and their midlife crises, running off to buy sports cars and date women way too young for them. Now I'm thinking about dating a man who is way too young for me."

"Is that what you think? That you're going through a midlife crisis?" He tried to keep the incredulity out of his voice, but it was difficult. Rhiannon was way too grounded to ever be accused of that.

"No, of course not. But that's what people will say about me." She paused. "Although, now that I think about it, most of those men would probably deny that they were going through one, as well.

"But, no. I had my crisis a few years ago. You have nothing to do with that."

"So what do I have to do with?"

She sucked in a deep breath, blew it out in a loud sigh. "I have absolutely no idea."

"Do you mind if I ask you a few questions, then? Maybe we can fumble around together for a while—just to find out where we stand."

She stiffened, her entire body going so rigid that he was shocked she could still sit. From the way she'd reacted, he expected her to tell him no, but in the end, she just nodded slowly.

"Does what people say about you really matter to you?"

"Doesn't it matter to you?"

He shook his head. "You know, it really doesn't. I think you're beautiful. Really, really beautiful—inside and out—and I feel lucky to be here with you. The fact that you're older than I am means nothing. Life is about the experiences you've had, not how many years you've lived. So far, I think we're pretty well-matched when it comes to that kind of stuff."

She didn't answer for the longest time, just gazed out over the water, watching as people kayaked next to them on the lake. "This thing between us. It's not going anywhere, right?"

He stiffened at the assumption. "What does that mean?"

"I mean, we're just in this to have some fun, right? It's nothing serious?"

"Does that matter?"

"Of course it does. You say eleven years is no big deal, but those are pretty big years between us. Marriage years. Child-bearing years. That makes a huge difference, doesn't it? Kind of puts things in perspective?"

"Rhiannon." He grabbed her hands in his and looked her directly in the eye. "Can't we both just take a deep breath and relax? I like you. I really like you and I hope you feel the same way about me. If you do, let's forget about everything else for a while and just see where this goes."

"That's just it. I can't forget about everything else. You say it doesn't matter, but it does. What are your friends going to say when they meet me? Your parents?"

"My friends are Neanderthals. They'll probably make jokes about how lucky I am to be with a woman in her sexual prime. And as for my parents, they've never cared about anything but me being happy."

"Oh, God! I hadn't even thought about the cougar jokes." She tugged her hand from his and rubbed it over her eyes. "This is *such* a bad idea."

"No, it's not. And you know it, or you wouldn't be here right now. So come on, what do you say? You want to try this thing for a few weeks, see how it works out?"

"I keep thinking it's not fair to you, Shawn," she blurted out as she bit her thumbnail down to the quick.

He wanted to kiss her right then, wanted to run his tongue over her abused thumb and soothe any wounds she might have inflicted on herself. But the last time he'd kissed her she'd taken off without so much as a "see you later," and he didn't relish jumping into Town Lake after her. So he contented himself with just watching her and hoping she'd figure out what she was doing and stop before she drew blood.

"Look," he said after watching her for a while. "I like you, Rhiannon. I like the deadpan sense of humor that slips out of you when I least expect it. I like the way you think, and the way you smile. I like the fact that you're here with me, now, even though I make you nervous. And I really, really like the way you smell, like the honeysuckle in my garden and rain on a sunny, summer afternoon."

She took a deep, trembling breath. "That's not fair. You're a writer—how am I supposed to compete with that?"

"Don't compete. Just tell me that you like me, too,

that you want to give this thing between us a try. I think we could have a lot of fun together."

"Fun?"

"I'm sure you've heard of the concept. It involves dating, hanging out, going to the movies, doing a bunch of cool things together."

"Oh, right. Fun. I have heard of that concept."

"So what do you say?"

She pretended to think about it, but he could see the sparkle in her eye and it made him happier than he could remember being in a very long time.

"I guess, I say okay."

"Yeah?"

"Yeah."

He couldn't stop the grin that split his face. "Excellent." Reaching for her hand, he pulled it to his mouth and placed a lingering kiss right in the center of her palm.

She gasped, trembled, her fingers curling into a loose fist. He started to say more, though he wasn't sure what words he would have used, when a bunch of people on the boat cried out and pointed at the sky.

Looking up, he held Rhiannon and watched as thousands upon thousands of bats flew out from under the Congress Street Bridge, wings flapping wildly as they spiraled up, up, up and into the night. For the first time since Cynthia had messed with his head all those years before, he didn't envy them their freedom to just fly away.

CHAPTER NINE

RHIANNON WAS NERVOUS as she and Shawn traversed the plank that led from the boat onto solid ground again. They'd only known each other a couple of weeks, but she'd already screwed up the thing between them at least once. She didn't want to do that again, any more than she wanted to lay her vulnerabilities out there for Shawn to see.

At the same time, she was sick of being poor Rhiannon, sick of being limited by her own expectations of herself. Maybe if she just did this—stepped outside of her comfort zone and went for it—maybe everything would work itself out. Or, barring that, maybe she would do just what Shawn had suggested. She'd have a little fun and let the future take care of itself.

It was an alien concept—at least, it had been for the past three years—but she was suddenly ready to give it a try. God knew, living the way she had been hadn't made her happy. Why shouldn't she try something new?

Not that she figured all of her hang-ups were going to be cured now that she had decided to date Shawn, but at least she was taking baby steps. Making progress. Refusing to be a victim any longer.

"So, how was your first bat cruise?" Shawn asked as they headed back up the trails to the street.

"It was really great. Thanks for taking me."

"Yeah, it was such a hardship."

She laughed. "Are you ever serious?"

"Only when forced to be. And even then, not so much. Serious isn't a good look on me."

"I don't know." She glanced at him from beneath her lashes. "I can't imagine anything not being a good look on you."

Shawn raised his eyebrows in mock surprise. "Are you flirting with me, Ms. Jenkins?"

She'd just been being honest, but maybe that was the wrong approach. It had been so long since she'd dated someone—almost eighteen years—that *rusty* didn't quite cover how she felt.

Deciding to go along with his easy banter, she said, "I just might be, Mr. Emerson. Why? Is that a problem?"

"Not at all. I just wanted to be sure I wasn't misreading the signals."

"You weren't." Rhiannon found she wasn't brave enough to look Shawn in the eye as she flirted with him, but she squeezed his hand to let him know she meant what she said.

"So, are you hungry?" he asked as they reached the street.

"Actually, I am," she said, surprised to find that it was true. She'd spent the past couple of years without much of an appetite, and now suddenly she was starving almost all of the time.

"Now that I think about it, I'm not sure I should feed you," he teased. "The last time I did, you ran off five minutes after dinner was finished."

She flushed. "I'm really sorry I did that. I just—"

"Hey, no sweat. I was just messing with you. I know this great Japanese place a couple of blocks away. Are you up for it?"

"Try to keep me away."

They feasted on sushi and tempura, chicken teriyaki and fried rice and for dessert, green-tea ice cream. Amazingly, Rhiannon ate every bit of the food that was put in front of her. It all tasted so good, though she wasn't sure if it was the food or the warmth and amusement in Shawn's eyes as he asked incessant questions about her family and her childhood, then teased her about her answers. It turned out he was the youngest in his family, the exact opposite of her, and that he had a big sister who pretty much felt it was her job to keep him in line—even now that he was almost thirty.

She found it kind of interesting to see things from the other side. She was so used to being the one who watched over her siblings that she'd forgotten how they sometimes viewed her with as much exasperation as she viewed them.

It had happened a lot less since the rape, as her family had a tendency to walk on eggshells around her now. But she had memories of being driven absolutely insane by her younger brother and sisters. It was vaguely comforting to realize that Shawn had the same reactions, though for very different reasons.

After she'd eaten as many bites of her ice cream as she could manage, Shawn escorted her out into the street. She resisted the urge to twirl around like a little girl in a princess dress, but that was exactly how she felt—like Cinderella at the ball, right before the clock struck midnight. A part of her was even waiting for the shoe to fall...

"I had a great time tonight," she murmured as the strolled along the still-busy downtown street.

"You say that like you think the date is over."

"Isn't it?" she asked uncertainly, discomfort overwhelming her lazy pleasure as she imagined what Shawn could have planned for the rest of the night. She might have decided she was ready for casual dating, but she wasn't ready for anything else. Not yet, certainly, and maybe not ever.

"Don't look so freaked out. I promise, there are no animal sacrifices or other illegal acts on the agenda for the rest of the night."

"Well, that's a shame," she replied, regaining her composure. "It's been a while since I've been to a good animal sacrifice."

He laughed. "Now *you're* scaring *me*."

"Don't worry." She reached out, patted his arm. "I'll be gentle."

"Oh, I'm not worried." His eyes went two shades deeper and suddenly the air between them was infused with sensual tension. She wanted to pull away, wanted to get closer, but didn't know how to do either. In the end, she stayed where she was, her gaze locked with his.

Shawn leaned in slowly, obviously giving her plenty of time to stop him—or to flee, as she had once before. But it turned out this time she wasn't going anywhere. Her need to be close to him outweighed everything else, even the fear that still ruled so much of her life. But this time, her feet were planted on the ground and the spinning in her stomach had a lot more to do with excitement than it did with fear.

Rhiannon braced herself for the feel of his lips on

hers, for the riot of emotions that had bombarded her last time. But at the last minute, Shawn turned his head and brushed his lips across her cheek. She didn't know if she was relieved or disappointed.

Probably a mixture of both, she thought wryly, even as she wondered when the disappointment would out-weigh the relief. Wondered if it ever would.

"Come on. I have one more place to take you tonight."

She started to ask him where they were going, then decided against it. Let him keep his surprise—the last one had been more than worth waiting for.

But when they stopped in front of a huge sports complex, she glanced at him, puzzled. "We're going to watch a kid's baseball game?"

"Nope. No game tonight." But he went through the front gate anyway.

"Well, if there's no game, then what are we doing here?"

"We're going to hit a few."

"Hit a few what?" she asked blankly.

"Balls." His wicked grin was back, the one he'd used to convince her to plan his party and check out his house and go on this date with him. "We're going to have a go at the batting cage."

Of course they were. Because, really, where else would Shawn Emerson finish up a date but at a kid's athletic complex? And how odd was it that she was actually excited by the prospect?

"Come on. You can pick out a bat while I get us a cage."

"You make it sound like we're at the zoo."

"That description isn't as far off as you might think, especially on Saturday mornings."

"Really? You spend enough time here to know that, hmm?"

"I coach a kids' baseball team. Our games are here on Saturday mornings, so I do spend more than my fair share of time here." He winked, then headed off to the cashier's booth at the front of the park.

She watched him go, bemused. Though she'd figured out that he was a big kid at heart, she never would have pictured Shawn as the type to donate his time to a kids' baseball league. Yet, the more that she thought about it, the less it surprised her. His gentle, generous treatment of her had already convinced her he was a stand-up guy.

She walked over to the bats and ran her hands over a few as she waited for him to come back. The sad fact was she wasn't overly skilled at softball, never had been—even in school. Which meant that she had no idea what she was testing the bats for. Though some felt heavier than others, she didn't have a clue which one would work for her.

When Shawn returned a couple of minutes later, she had picked out a shiny blue-and-silver bat. "Is that the one you like the feel of?" he asked curiously.

"I don't know. I picked it because it was pretty."

"Not a big baseball fan?"

"I don't mind watching it, but I think I was fourteen and in Freshman P.E. the last time I held a bat. I can't say I've missed it."

Shawn picked up a few bats, wrapped his hands around their bases and held them up as if he was actually going to hit a ball with them. "So, that's what you meant by testing them?" she asked.

"Yeah. What did you think I meant?"

She shrugged. "I didn't have a clue."

"We're going to change all that." He held a bat out to her. "Here, try this one."

"It's not as pretty as the one I chose."

"True, but the one you picked is meant for a ten-year-old kid. You're a little too tall for it."

"Oh."

"Yeah. Now, come on. I promise to go easy on you."

"I've heard that before."

"No doubt."

But as Shawn led her to a nearby batting cage and cued up the ball machine, Rhiannon found herself looking forward to taking a turn at bat. While softball had never been her sport, she'd spent most of her life swimming and playing tennis. She hadn't done either in the past couple of years—hadn't done much of anything to be completely honest—and for the first time, she found herself missing the thrill of physical activity. There was something to be said for the feel of well-used muscles at the end of a workout session.

"Now, hitting a ball really isn't that hard," Shawn said as he lined her up directly across from the batting machine.

"They sure make it look hard in the major leagues." She held her bat to her shoulder and got ready to hit.

"That's because they're trying to hit off professional pitchers. I've got the machine set on slow pitches, so you shouldn't have any problem." He took a step back, looked at her, then shook his head with a laugh. "Okay, you wouldn't have any problem if you actually knew how to hold a bat."

"I know how to hold a bat!" she exclaimed, insulted.

"If you say so." He moved behind her and placed his hands on her hips. Her heart started beating triple-time, and the urge to flee—and to fight—was so strong within her that it took all her concentration not to act on it.

It's okay, she told herself. *It's just Shawn. You're safe. You're fine. It's just Shawn. He won't hurt you. You're safe.* She repeated the words to herself over and over again until they became her mantra, the one thing she could hold on to as the world around her pitched and rocked.

"You'll have a much better shot of hitting the ball if you turn a little more to your right," Shawn continued, oblivious to her panic. She must be getting better at hiding the freak-outs—six months before, there was no way anyone could have missed her as she started to lose it.

"Now, choke up a little on the bat…" He continued speaking in a slow, easy tone that did more to ease her worry than anything else could have and by the time he finally moved away from her, Rhiannon not only had herself back under control, but she had a pretty decent batting stance, as well.

"I'm going to turn the machine on now," Shawn called as he headed toward the other side of the cage. "Just relax and let yourself swing at the pitches. Have fun."

Squatting down like he'd told her, Rhiannon held the bat up and prepared to connect with the ball as the machine fired. She waited, waited, then swung right when the ball was in what Shawn referred to as "the sweet spot." She waited to hear the crack of bat meeting ball, and was shocked when she realized the ball had hit the fence behind her.

"That's okay. Don't worry about it. Try swinging about one second earlier."

She did as he suggested, and still the ball soared right by her. Again and again, until Rhiannon was sweaty and more than a little frustrated and Shawn was trying his best not to laugh.

"Maybe baseball's not your game," he said with a grin. "We can go do something else if you'd like."

"Turn the machine back on," she snapped. "I'm going to hit one of these balls if it kills me."

"Are you sure? I didn't mean to—"

She glared at him. "Are you going to turn that thing back on or am I?"

"All right, all right. But maybe you should loosen up a little, take off your coat. It's a bit tight and might be preventing you from swinging through."

"Yeah, that's what's preventing me from hitting. My too-tight coat, not my complete lack of talent at the sport."

"Still. Try it and see if it helps. God knows, it couldn't hurt."

She narrowed her eyes at him, even as she shrugged out of her coat and tossed it on the ground. "You know, payback's a bitch."

"I'm looking forward to it."

She grabbed the bat and got ready to hit, or try to hit. "Go ahead. Turn that stupid thing back on."

But Shawn didn't move, didn't so much as acknowledge that he'd heard her. Wondering what had distracted him, she followed his gaze with her own, then cursed under her breath as she realized that *she* was what had distracted him. At least her scars had. She'd gotten so caught up in the game that she'd forgotten herself, had stripped down to the thin silk tank top she wore under her suit and now her scar-riddled arms were on display for the whole world to see.

For Shawn to see.

She waited for him to say something, to ask her how she'd damaged her skin so severely, but he didn't say a word. He just stared at her for long seconds, his eyes surveying the damage. Then he turned away and flipped the switch on the ball machine.

"Get ready," he said. "The balls will start in a minute."

How could she get ready when she was imploding? Crumbling? He was the first person to see her scars in nearly a year, the first person besides her doctors and family—and Logan—to *ever* see them. How could she have been so careless? How could she have forgotten herself so completely?

A ball whipped past her, one she hadn't even bothered to try to swing at.

"Rhiannon," Shawn called, his voice unusually firm. "Swing the bat—you're going to end up getting hit by one of these balls if you're not careful."

"I don't want to do this anymore," she said, dropping the bat onto the Astroturf. She knew she sounded like a spoiled child, but she didn't care. Couldn't care. All she wanted was to escape.

She reached for her suit jacket, shrugged into it quickly. It was stupid—the damage had already been done—but staying in just her shirt wasn't an option. She was far too vulnerable that way. Far too exposed.

"Rhiannon."

She reached for her coat and purse. "Can we go?"

"Rhiannon." He jogged over to her, tried to touch her but she shrugged him off.

"I have an early meeting tomorrow that I forgot about. I should get home and prep for it a little before bed." She started walking away.

"Rhiannon, stop."

"Stop what?" Her smile was brittle when she turned to him. "Stop talking? Stop caring about my job? Stop…" Her voice broke and she turned away, determined that she would not embarrass herself in front of Shawn any further.

He grabbed her elbow, turned her until she was facing him. "Stop pushing me away."

"I can't. I'm sorry, but I just can't."

CHAPTER TEN

SHAWN WAS FURIOUS—COLDLY, horribly furious. So furious that he could barely concentrate on driving. So furious that he could barely think.

He took the corner leading to the main drag that surrounded Lake Travis much too fast, the back wheels of his Audi skidding as he tried to stay on the road. Swearing, he slowed down—there was no use driving like a maniac. It wouldn't erase the hurt in Rhiannon's eyes any more than it would take away the rage burning in his gut.

Someone had hurt Rhiannon, badly enough to scar. And then Shawn had hurt her again, by staring at the scars she had unconsciously revealed.

He hated that he'd upset her, hated more that she thought he was repulsed by her when nothing could be further from the truth. Even as he'd stared, he'd known he should look away, known he should pretend that the scars were no big deal. But he hadn't been able to do that—not when all he could think about was how she'd gotten them.

Not when he'd been able to picture some asshole hurting her, again and again.

Had her husband done that to her? Is that why she'd gotten divorced, why she was so wary of men? Or had some other bastard—

His hands clenched the steering wheel. He didn't know what to do, didn't know how to handle the emotions ripping through him. Ever since childhood, when he'd realized how impotent anger really was, he'd refused to let himself get into this state. When things got rough, he'd always made a point of disconnecting, of going around the roadblocks instead of trying to fight his way through them. Life was so much easier when you dodged and weaved around the unpleasantness. Even more so if you walked away before things got bad to begin with.

He broke out in a cold sweat at the idea of walking away from Rhiannon. At the same time, he wasn't sure he could stick it out, either. Not because he was repulsed by her scars, but because they reminded him so much of Cynthia's scars that it completely freaked him out. Of course, Rhiannon's weren't self-inflicted—from their placement, he could see that most of them, if not all of them, were defensive wounds. Unlike Cynthia's, whose scars were the result of years of suicide attempts.

When he'd gotten involved with Cynthia, he hadn't known how sick she was, hadn't known she was sick at all, actually. So when he'd had to run her to the hospital to get her stomach pumped after she'd overdosed on Tylenol, he'd been shocked—but determined to stand by her.

Her need for self-destruction hadn't stopped there. When the doctors saved her for what turned out to be the third time, she'd taken to cutting herself instead. He'd lived with it for nearly two and a half years—the depression, the anxiety, the incredible moodiness—before she'd finally succeeded in dying.

It had been nearly six years since Cynthia had killed herself, but he could still see her scars clearly—inside and out.

He didn't think he could watch another woman battle problems so serious he couldn't come close to understanding them. He'd wanted to help Cynthia and had ended up nearly dying himself, from guilt and heartbreak.

The idea of doing it with Rhiannon, too, was almost more than he could bear.

Of course, he might not have a choice in the matter. Rhiannon had walked away from him tonight without a backward glance and he wasn't sure how he was ever going to get her to talk to him again—if he even decided that was what he wanted.

As they'd left the batting cage, he'd tried to explain, had tried to tell her that he didn't care about her scars—at least not the way she thought—but she hadn't wanted to listen to him. Had refused to hear what he was saying. Instead, she'd politely thanked him for dinner and started walking toward her office as fast as her classy pumps could carry her.

He'd insisted on walking her back to her car—it was dark, after all, and they were downtown. There was no way he was going to let anything else happen to her. But the entire way he'd been more than conscious of the fact that she didn't want him there, that she was putting up with his escort because it was easier than arguing with him. Gone was the easy camaraderie they had shared earlier in the evening, only to be replaced by a wall of frigid silence he didn't have a clue how to bridge. It had taken him a hell of a lot of work just to get Rhiannon to actually consent to go on a date with him—and that was before he'd stared at something that she was totally self-conscious about.

Could he have been a bigger idiot?

He was so wrapped up in his thoughts that he nearly missed the turnoff to his street and ended up skidding again, despite his vow to be more cautious. Shit, at this rate he would be lucky to make it home without wrapping his car around a tree—just one more reason it was a bad idea to open yourself up and care about someone else. When they got to you, really got to you, it messed you up.

As soon as he pulled into the garage, he was out of the car and slamming toward the house. Every instinct he had told him to call Rhiannon, to try to apologize to her one more time. But something held him back. Maybe it was the fact that he figured an apology like the one he owed her was better delivered in person than over the phone. More likely, it was the feeling that he was in quicksand and slowly sinking.

After having spent almost three years bogged down in an emotional quagmire, he just didn't think he could handle it again. Better to stay way from Rhiannon until he decided if he could handle what she'd been through.

But he didn't know *what* she'd been through—that was the problem. He'd been close enough to her to recognize that the scars she had hadn't been caused by fire or accident. Their placement was too deliberate—someone had done that to her, had cut her with something over and over again. And the wide scars on her wrists… He didn't want to dwell on what might have caused those. Already his suspicions were nearly driving him crazy.

Though he knew it was probably a violation of her trust—not that she exactly trusted him at this point—he settled down in front of his computer and typed Rhiannon's name and Austin, Texas, into the search engine. He didn't know if he would find anything, but he had to try. The look on her face when she'd realized that she had exposed her scars—exposed herself—had wounded him more than anything had in longer than he could remember.

The first few hits all linked her to Parties by L.K. and he skimmed through them without paying much attention. But somewhere in the middle of the second page, Shawn realized that all of the entries suddenly belonged to the *Austin American-Statesman* and the Associated Press. Clicking on a few, he stared in confusion as byline after byline came up for Rhiannon Jenkins.

She'd been a reporter? He clicked on another story, hoping to find a picture of her somewhere. Maybe there was more than one Rhiannon Jenkins in Austin—though her first name wasn't common, her last name was far from exotic. That had to be the case, because it didn't make sense that she'd just stopped being a reporter one day and become an event planner instead. Not judging by the size and scope of the stories she'd covered for the paper, and then for the AP.

This Rhiannon Jenkins had covered everything from political scandals in Texas's capitol to major decisions from the 5th Circuit Court of Appeals. She had covered murder trials and major missing person cases, had uncovered a scandal that stretched from the boardrooms of two major Austin corporations to the halls of Washington. And she had dropped off the face of the earth nearly eleven months before the first hit that placed Rhiannon at her current job.

Somehow he strongly doubted that that was a coincidence.

Which meant what? Rhiannon had been a reporter—a very good reporter—for years and had suddenly walked away to become a party planner? It didn't make sense, especially with the nearly year-long gap between her last article for the AP and her first mention at Parties by L.K.

What had she been doing for those months, he wondered? Taking time off to get over a divorce? Healing from the attack of an abusive husband?

Turning his attention away from speculation about Rhiannon and back to the computer screen in front of him, Shawn metaphorically rolled up his sleeves and then set about finding out everything he could about Rhiannon. The next time he saw her, there was no way he was going to chance hurting her out of ignorance. One time was more than enough for that.

But three hours later, he finally gave up. If there was something else to be found about Rhiannon—besides the Pulitzer prize she'd won at thirty-one and the public announcement of her divorce from a Richard McCarthy, he couldn't find it. But just because it wasn't public record didn't mean it hadn't happened. He just had to figure out where to look.

Walking into the bathroom, he turned on the faucet and splashed cold water on his face in an effort to clarify things in his own brain. It didn't work. Nothing was clear, nothing was how he'd expected it to be.

Sure, he'd assumed Rhiannon's wariness had stemmed from somewhere, but not physical abuse. Not abuse that left those kinds of scars. It was a nightmare and he hated the fact that he'd pursued Rhiannon only to push her away now because he couldn't deal.

But the more he thought about it, the more he figured out that he couldn't do this again. He couldn't, wouldn't, deliberately hook up with a woman who had the power to destroy him with her own pain.

His past would not repeat itself—he wouldn't let it.

HUMILIATION WAS A JAGGED blade scraping away at her insides as Rhiannon poured herself a glass of wine. Normally she wasn't much of a drinker—it had been a little too easy to rely on alcohol to help her sleep after the attack, so she'd quit touching the stuff—but tonight she felt like she more than deserved it. God knew, her first foray into the dating arena in more than fifteen years hadn't gone quite the way she'd planned.

What had she been thinking? she wondered, as she walked through the dark living room toward her bedroom. How could she have forgotten herself so completely that she'd *taken off her jacket in front of him?* It wasn't like she didn't live with the scars every day of her life, wasn't like she ever forgot that they were there.

Except she had forgotten. Today, with Shawn, the pain of the past few years had dropped away until it had been just the two of them having fun. Until she was just regular old Rhiannon Jenkins, on a date with a smart, nice, good-looking man. For a minute, she'd even thought she had a chance of hitting that stupid ball.

But instead of a home run, she'd ended up striking

out in the worst way possible. It would be a long time before she forgot the look in his eyes when he'd seen her arms. It was eerily similar to the way Richard had eventually looked at her.

Lifting her glass to her lips, she drained the wine in one quick gulp, then started undressing as the alcohol burned warmly in her stomach. Normally she undressed in the dark, hating to look at the damage that had been done to her body, but tonight she couldn't help herself.

Making her way into the bathroom, Rhiannon flipped on the light and forced herself to stand in front of the full-length mirror. She'd already taken off her jacket, so she was dressed only in her blue silk tank and black dress pants. Her arms were bare, the curlicue scars on them standing out in stark relief against the faint olive tint of her skin.

They weren't atrocious, she realized with a faint sense of surprise. It had been so long since she'd looked at them—since she'd allowed herself to look at them—that she hadn't realized how much the scars that crisscrossed her biceps and forearms had faded. They were still there, obviously, or Shawn wouldn't have been able to see them from across the batting cage, but at least they were no longer that ugly pinkish-purple she'd lived with for so long.

No, the scars were now nothing but thin, white lines that looped and crossed down her shoulder to her biceps and triceps, past her elbows to her forearms. They could almost pass for lace or the thinnest of ribbon if one discounted the complete randomness of the pattern. Or the wide scars around her wrists, from where she'd yanked against the ropes until her blood had stained them dark red.

He'd done it to mark her, so that she would always remember him—or at least that's what he'd told her. Personally, she thought he'd done it because he was a sadistic bastard, who'd enjoyed causing as much pain as he possibly could.

Maybe they were both right, because God knew, most nights his face was still the last thing she saw before drifting off to sleep and the first thing she remembered after waking up.

Three years later and she still didn't know what had made him do what he'd done to her. It wasn't just that he'd beat and cut her damn near to death, nor was it that he'd raped her. Both crimes were horrendous in and of themselves, but together... She shuddered. Together they had ruined any chance at a life she would ever have.

But standing here thinking about it, thinking about *him,* wasn't getting the job done. Inside her head a voice was shrieking at her to stop, to walk away. Not to do this. But a part of her knew that if she didn't do this now, she never would. And she was sick of living like that.

Sick of hiding behind long sleeves and pants in the summertime and long, matronly dresses at the parties she oversaw.

Sick of showering and dressing in the dark because she couldn't stand to see her own body.

With a shudder, Rhiannon closed her eyes. Ripped off her shirt. Stepped out of her pants. Took off her bra and panties, until she stood completely nude in front of the mirror. Then tried to look, tried to force herself to open her eyes and confront the woman she had become.

It was even harder than she thought it would be. Images of the dark, unreadable look in Shawn's eyes as he'd stared mixed with the face of the man who had done this to her until it was all she could do not to dive into bed and pull the covers over her head.

But she'd already done that, had already spent days and weeks hiding from the world, letting her life pass her by because she was too depressed to deal. Too miserable to get on with a life that felt like it was no longer worth living.

Damn it, no. She forced her eyes open. She was finished hiding from herself, finished hating herself and her body because of what some madman had done to her. Though everything inside of her urged her to flee, Rhiannon held her ground and made herself look.

She started with her legs, which bore scars similar to those on her arms—wide bands around her ankles from the restraints, and shallow knife wounds on her shins and thighs, from where he had cut her and laughed.

Then she moved up to her breasts and abdomen, where deeper, wider scars marked where he had stabbed her—not deeply enough to kill her, but more than deeply enough to mark her for life.

Memories bombarded her, making her knees tremble and her breath hitch. She pushed them away, refused to give in to the fear that assailed her every time she thought of him. Oh, but it was hard, so hard to stand here, and look at the damage. To look at what he'd done to her simply because he could.

When she'd had enough, when her knees had finally stopped knocking together and her heartbeat had almost returned to normal, she flipped off the light and made her way back into the bedroom.

After crawling into her pajamas, she burrowed under her covers but left the light on. Across the room, the TV beckoned, promising if not total oblivion then at least a momentary distraction. She reached for the remote, started to click the power button, but in the end, couldn't do it.

That's how she'd been coping for years. A sleeping pill combined with late-night reruns of her favorite sitcoms. Anything and everything to avoid the fact that she'd been hurt, simply because someone had wanted to hurt her, to scare her.

Anything and everything to avoid the fact that her husband had left her to deal with the aftermath of the attack on her own—all because he couldn't accept what she had become. But then, it was hard to blame him when she couldn't accept it herself.

Reaching out, she swept the empty wineglass off of her nightstand with one quick flick of her hand. It hit the wall and shattered into a million tiny pieces, irreparably broken, like her.

It felt so good to admit it, so good not to fight it anymore that she shoved the pile of books onto the floor next. Then her phone and alarm clock.

Rage swelled within her. Huge, towering, uncontainable rage that nearly smothered her with its intensity. Climbing out of bed, she grabbed the large, freestanding jewelry box Richard had given her for her thirty-fifth birthday and shoved it hard enough for it to tumble onto its side. The mirrored tray she kept on top of it came crashing down, along with her perfume bottles and hand creams. Its doors fell open, earrings and rings, bracelets and brooches, necklaces and watches tumbling drunkenly out.

She knew she should stop, knew she should crawl back into bed and pull the covers over her head like she had so many times before. But she was sick of hiding, sick of pretending all those horrible things hadn't happened to her. They had happened, and damn it, she was furious about it.

Rhiannon headed for the dresser on the other side of the room, picked up the beautiful vase she'd bought at her favorite furniture store and smashed it against the wood. Did the same to the tall, slender lamp and collection of odds and ends that rested on the dresser's other side. Then picked up the music box Matt had given her the previous year and heaved it, as hard as she could, against the wall. It hit a print she had hanging there, under glass, and both shattered, the picture frame crashing to the ground with a resounding thud.

She moved on to the chest of drawers near the door and did the same thing, until there was nothing left to throw. Nothing left in the entire room to destroy.

When she was finished, when the fury departed as suddenly as it had come, Rhiannon stepped gingerly through the mess. Closing her bedroom door firmly behind her, she sank onto the sofa and pulled the lavender afghan she had resting there over her. For the first time in a very long time, she fell asleep almost as soon as she closed her eyes.

CHAPTER ELEVEN

EVEN THOUGH SHE'D SWORN to herself that she was done with Shawn, sitting on a lounge chair in her brother's backyard, watching Matt flip burgers and flirt with his wife, Camille, it was hard for Rhiannon not to think of him. Harder still not to think of everything she was missing as she cradled Matt's newborn son, Cole, in her arms.

He'd burst into the world six weeks before with bright blue eyes and a full head of auburn hair and from the second she'd held him, Rhiannon had been one hundred percent in love. Cole was the first baby any of her siblings had had, the baby that had finally made her an aunt after she'd spent so many years longing to be a mother.

She loved his warm weight in her arms, loved his delicate rosebud mouth and his wide, alert eyes that were even now staring up at her with wonder. Loved everything about him from the tips of his tiny toes to the top of his little head. And she couldn't help wondering what it would be like if the attack had never happened, if she and Richard had gone through with their plans to finally have a baby of their own. She'd wanted one for so long, but had always let him put her off. There was never enough time, enough money, enough anything.

She had finally convinced him to start trying a

month or so before she'd been raped, and had spent hours daydreaming about what it would feel like to hold her own baby in her arms. That had been one more dream that had crashed and burned the day she'd been ambushed by a madman.

Cole burped, and a trickle of milk leaked from the corner of his mouth. Reaching for the burp cloth Camille made sure was never far from the baby, Rhiannon cleaned him up before lifting him to her shoulder and rubbing soothing circles on his back.

"I can take him if you want."

She glanced up to find her sister-in-law watching her, an easy and relaxed smile on the other woman's face. "That's okay." Rhiannon smiled. "I love to hold him. Go hang out with Matt for a while—I'm sure you two don't get much time together these days."

"Yes, well, I've been banished from the grill." Camille popped the top off a soda and handed it to Rhiannon before opening another one for herself. "Apparently, I'm too much of a distraction."

Rhiannon could believe it. She was shocked at how good her sister-in-law looked six weeks after giving birth—currently, she was dressed in a skimpy pair of cutoff jeans and a tank top that showed off the fact that she'd already lost most of the baby weight. Plus, her skin was glowing and she had a huge smile on her face. Only the dark circles under her eyes told the tale of how little sleep she'd been getting lately.

"So, what's been going on with you?" Camille asked as she settled back in the lounge chair next to Rhiannon's. "Planning any cool parties lately?"

She felt heat crawl into her face and prayed Camille wouldn't notice. Keeping her voice steady was an effort, but she managed to do it long enough to say, "I'm working on a few things. One of them is really cool—a sixtieth wedding anniversary, if you can believe that. They were seventeen when they got married and they've made it for longer than half a century."

"That is amazing. Sometimes I wonder if Matt and I will even make it to our first anniversary. After our rocky start sometimes I feel like we're still really getting to know each other."

Rhiannon sat up straighter. "Why? Are you guys having problems again?"

"No, nothing like that. Things are great. It's just, marriage is hard, you know?"

"Absolutely. It's really hard."

"And yet I wouldn't give him up. He drives me nuts, but I love him and Cole more than I'd ever imagined it was possible to love anyone."

Rhiannon froze, her whole world kind of caving in around her as she listened to Camille wax poetic about her new family.

It sucked, really sucked, that she would never have that. At the same time, if the night before had taught her nothing else, it had taught her that she needed to be content with what she had. A new career that she liked. An extended family that she was crazy about. A nephew that she adored.

It was enough, especially considering the state she'd been in two years before. She'd had no husband, no job, no way of interacting with the world around her. She'd come a long way and pushing for more was just foolhardy.

"Well, enough about the gripes of a newly married

woman," Camille said with a grin. "Tell me more about the fabulous parties you're planning."

"There's not much else going on. I am doing a carnival-type theme for another client—"

"A carnival? With games and everything?"

"That's what I'm hoping for." She concentrated on the party, did her best to forget Shawn's part in it. "The whole thing will be based around a movie theme. The client just sold the movie rights to his graphic novel character and wants to impress a bunch of the Hollywood types that will be in town for the film festival next month."

"That sounds like a lot of fun."

"It should be—if I can bring it in under budget. He gave me a really large one to work with, but I keep having new brain waves and brain waves cost money."

"You keep having new ideas because it's a great concept. Really original—I would love to go to a party like that and can't imagine that a bunch of actors and directors wouldn't, as well. I hope he's not giving you too hard of a time."

"It's not like that." Rhiannon felt her practiced smile start to freeze and turned her face away, hoping Camille wouldn't notice.

But her sister-in-law had eyes like an eagle, and before Rhiannon could think of a way to divert Camille's attention, she was leaning forward in her chair, eyes narrowed. "You look funny. Why do you look funny?"

"I don't!"

"Really, because from where I'm sitting it looks like you just ate a very big, very nasty-looking bug."

"That's disgusting!"

"Yeah, well, if the shoe fits—"

"Hey, mind if we join you guys?" Rhiannon glanced up to find her friend Sarah standing there, her one-year-old son in her arms while her not-quite-three-year-old daughter clutched her pant leg. Sarah was the wife of Matt's partner, Reece, and she and Rhiannon had been friends for a number of years.

"Not at all," she answered, grateful for the distraction.

"Hey, Rosie, why don't you take that ball to Daddy and your brothers?" Sarah suggested as she settled herself and her son in a nearby chair. "I'm sure they and Uncle Matt would love to play with you."

"Ball?" Rosie asked around the two fingers she had jammed into her mouth.

"See it? It's right next to that plant." Sarah pointed.

"I get ball, Mommy!" Rosie ran toward the beach ball on chubby legs, the bells tied to her shoes jingling with every step she took.

"Good girl, Rosie."

They all watched as Rosie took off toward her father and the twin boys from Sarah's first marriage, as fast as her little legs could carry her. But once she reached Reece, Sarah turned her attention to Rhiannon. "Okay, spill."

"Spill what?"

"You looked like you were going to puke when I came over here and I want to know what's up. Are you okay?"

"Nothing's up." Rhiannon's cheeks started burning and she cursed her stupid redheaded complexion.

Sarah raised one blond eyebrow at Camille. "If she won't tell me, you had better."

"Actually, I was just trying to pry it out of her." Camille took a long drink of her soda. "We were talking about a party she's planning for a local graphic novelist and suddenly she started to look sick."

"Really?" It was Sarah's turn to lean forward, even as she popped a bottle in her son's mouth. "So he's single, then. Is he hot?"

"I never said anything about Shawn being single *or* hot."

Cole started to whimper, turning to root around on Rhiannon's breast, and Camille reached for him with a grin. "You didn't have to, honey. It's written all over your face."

Rhiannon pressed her newly freed hands to her cheeks. "No, it isn't. Nothing's going on between us."

"I think she's protesting too much, don't you, Sarah?"

"I think so." Sarah slipped the bottle from her sleeping son's mouth, then reached into her bag and grabbed a blanket to tuck around him. "So, tell us about him."

"There's nothing to tell. He hired me to plan a party and I'm planning it."

"Yet you don't freak out when you talk about your other clients. Come on, Rhiannon," Camille wheedled. "We're old married ladies. We need to live vicariously through you."

"I'm older than both of you."

"Yeah, but you're single and hot and really smart. Guys go for that."

"This whole conversation is ridiculous. He's one of those guys who's never serious, who's always joking around. I mean, he draws cartoons for a living!" Even as she spoke, Rhiannon couldn't help wondering if she was lying to herself. After all, Shawn had been extremely serious when he'd driven her back to her office after their disastrous date.

"You said he wrote graphic novels," Sarah corrected.

"Is there a difference? I mean, his career choice is to draw pictures of men in tights and capes!"

"There is absolutely a difference," Camille chastised softly. "One of my friends has been trying for years to get his graphic novel picked up. It's a grueling industry and very few people are good enough to make the cut."

"Not to mention the fact that if he's doing well enough to afford a party like the one you described, it must be a pretty good career," added Sarah.

"I know it is. I didn't mean to make it sound like I don't respect what he does. I do. It's just that I get the feeling that he's never grown up. That life's one big game to him, you know? He has every video-game console known to man hooked up to his TV, not to mention the built-in basketball court in his backyard. Plus he's always joking around—it's hard to get a straight answer from him."

"That's not such a bad thing, you know, especially in a fling," Sarah mused. "I like a guy who can loosen up and have some fun."

"And yet you married Reece, who is wound so tight it's a miracle he doesn't bounce?"

"Hey, Reece can be fun. You just have to dig a little to get to it."

"Yeah, well, you don't have to dig to find Shawn's

frivolous side. It's right there for the whole world to see. He has huge, antique video games—that he still plays—in the middle of his family room, for God's sake."

"So what? Matt has a pile of video games ten feet high for his gaming system. Guys love that kind of stuff." Camille tilted her head and the purple streaks she'd added after the baby was born glinted in the sunlight. Rhiannon wondered what it would be like to be that self-confident, that comfortable in her own skin. She had been once, but the past few years had made remembering the woman she used to be almost impossible.

"I think you should give him a shot. He may not be husband material—"

"I'm not looking for a husband!"

"That's exactly what I'm saying," Camille continued. "Why don't you just take things slow, see where they go? It could be a lot of fun."

"I never said I was interested in Shawn."

"Yeah, but you never said you weren't. Right, Sarah?"

Rhiannon couldn't believe she was having this conversation, especially with Sarah and Camille. Unlike some of her other friends who had tried to set her up after the divorce—despite her protests that she wasn't ready—neither one of them had ever so much as mentioned a man to her. Now, suddenly, they were encouraging her to jump into bed with a perfect stranger. It was almost surreal.

"Stop. This whole discussion is ridiculous. It's not like he's even interested in me." He might have been once, but the look on his face when he'd stared at her scars had told her all she needed to know about what Shawn wanted, or didn't want, from her.

Camille snorted. "What's not to be interested in? You're smart, funny, gorgeous—"

"And I have enough baggage to fill up the luggage compartment of a 747. Not to mention I'm way older than he is."

Camille's eyes rounded. "You're older than he is? How much older?"

"He's still in his twenties."

"His twenties?" Sarah repeated, mouth agape.

"Well, almost thirty. And I'll be forty in a few days. Now do you see why this whole conversation is completely crazy?"

"Crazy like a fox, maybe. Go, Rhiannon." Camille curled her legs underneath her as she nursed the baby. "I think younger men are totally sexy."

"Oh, really?" asked Matt, eyebrows raised, as he walked by, carrying a tray heaped high with burgers. "Exactly what younger man do you find so sexy?"

"Oh, not for me. I'm fond of tall, dark and serious architect types myself."

"Good. Let's keep it that way." He laid the platter of food on a nearby table, then leaned down and kissed Camille warmly. Very warmly, and Camille seemed to be enjoying every second of it.

"So," Matt asked, when he finally raised his head. "If you aren't considering leaving me for a hot, younger guy…" He raised his eyebrows at Sarah. "Should I tell Reece he has some competition?"

"Oh, please, as if. We're talking about Rhiannon."

The look of sardonic amusement slid from Matt's

face and was replaced by one of complete and utter shock. "Are you dating again?"

She tried not to be offended by the total incredulity in his voice, told herself that Matt had been with her through everything and had seen how devastated she'd been—first by the attack and then by Richard walking out on her. He was probably just surprised at the idea of her looking for another man.

Not that she was looking, she reminded herself. It was all just silly conjecture on Camille's and Sarah's parts. But still, did her brother have to look like he'd just been poleaxed? Was she really so repulsive that he couldn't imagine a man being interested in her?

Annoyance—and maybe a bit of fear that he was right—made her voice sharper than she intended when she answered, "No. Of course not."

"Why of course not?" Camille demanded, and not for the first time Rhiannon wished her friend wasn't so good at picking up on things.

"Because, as I was telling you before, Shawn's a client. He's just some guy I met through work, not someone I'm planning on dating."

"Are you sure?" her brother demanded. "Because if you are, I have a friend who's a detective. I can get him to check this guy out "

"No one is checking anybody out. There's nothing *to* check out."

Camille elbowed Matt and he ran a frustrated hand over his face before turning back to Rhiannon. "Look, I'm not trying to tell you what to do, I just don't want to see you get hurt again."

"First of all, nothing's going on, so I can't get hurt. And secondly, why do you assume I'm *going* to get hurt again? Like I can't take care of myself because something crappy once happened to me?" she asked, unable to stop herself. While she was desperately afraid to get involved in another relationship, even a superficial one, it was terrible to realize that her brother might see just how badly off she really was, especially since she'd worked so hard to hide it from him.

"I don't, Rhiannon. I promise, I don't see you like that at all. It's just—" He paused, ran a hand through his hair in frustration. "After everything went down, you were a mess, Rhiannon, broken into so many pieces that I couldn't imagine you ever being able to fit them together again. I just don't want to see you end up back there again."

"I'm not going back there, I promise. My life isn't what I expected it to be, but that doesn't mean I don't like where I'm at." She mouthed the platitudes without thinking, but as she thought about them, she realized they were true. While there was still a bunch of things she wanted to change about her life, there were some things she would never mess with.

She liked being an event coordinator, liked planning strange and different parties. And she loved her family and friends. There might only be a few people that she trusted now, but she trusted them implicitly. Surely that counted for something.

She was tired of being a victim—in everyone's eyes. Sick to death of being "poor Rhiannon." Sick to death of being the one everyone worried about or talked about at parties.

"I didn't mean that—" The very real agitation in Matt's voice had her leaning over and patting his cheek. It was a gesture that drove him nuts and there was definitely still enough big sister in her to make the action worthwhile.

But later, as she was walking Cole around the backyard, cooing at him and making baby noises, her brother's words came back to her—along with her determination not to be a burden any longer.

She glanced around, trying to get a sense of where everyone was. Sarah and Reece were playing with their kids near the swimming pool while Matt and Camille were taking advantage of the time they had alone to cuddle on one of the loungers.

She'd been about to return the baby, but stopped dead when she saw them. They looked so good together, so quiet, so peaceful, that she didn't want to disturb them. So she hung back for a few minutes, admiring the way they were content just to hold each other.

Rhiannon wasn't sure how long she stood there watching her brother and sister-in-law—probably only a few seconds. But it was long enough to recognize the envy tightening her stomach. She didn't begrudge Matt and Camille the happiness they had found, but she missed it. Missed that sense of being part of a couple. Missed the touching, the support, the feeling that there was somebody in the world she belonged with and who belonged with her.

Richard may have been less than kind in the end, but for much of their relationship he'd been a good husband, friend and lover. The fact that things had gone so terribly wrong at the finish didn't negate what they had once had. What she was only just now beginning to realize she would someday like to have again.

Out of nowhere, Shawn's face rose up in front of her. She'd spent the past week staring at the phone and wondering if he would call. He never did, and while she told herself it had a lot more to do with her behavior than it did her scars, she wasn't so sure that was the truth.

She'd vowed to stop thinking of him numerous times throughout the week, but that didn't mean he didn't come to her—like now—in weird moments when she dropped her guard. Though this instant didn't seem like an ideal time for him to appear—at almost eleven years her junior, it wasn't like he was life-partner material.

And yet, she missed him. Missed the way he smiled at her. Missed the way he goofed around. Missed the way he was so much fun to be with. So much of her life was work—not just her job, but everything else, too.

More often than not, interacting with her friends and family was a chore because they either expected her to be completely healed or they wanted her to still be the victim they remembered from two and a half years before. She no longer felt like either, and trying to navigate the waters was exhausting at best.

Not to mention the fact that no matter how hard she tried, some days it was still nearly impossible to get out of bed in the morning.

But being with Shawn wasn't like that. It wasn't work. It wasn't simple—certainly not as simple as she had first thought—but it wasn't difficult, either. It was just nice.

When she closed her eyes at night, she could still see the way he'd looked at her arms that night at the batting cage. But as she gained a little distance, and a little perspective, she was beginning to realize that the look on his face hadn't been disgust so much as shock and concern. And while she'd had enough of

FREE Merchandise is 'in the Cards' for you!

Dear Reader,

We're giving away FREE MERCHANDISE!

Seriously, we'd like to reward you for reading this novel by giving you **FREE MERCHANDISE** worth over **$20**. And no purchase is necessary!

You see the Jack of Hearts sticker above? Paste that sticker in the box on the Free Merchandise Voucher inside. Return the Voucher promptly...and we'll send you valuable Free Merchandise!

Thanks again for reading one of our novels—and enjoy your Free Merchandise with our compliments!

Pam Powers

Pam Powers

P.S. Look inside to see what Free Merchandise is **"in the cards"** for you!

(H-SR-12/10)

W

e'd like to send you two free books to introduce you to the Harlequin® Superromance® series. These books are worth over $10, but they are yours to keep absolutely FREE! We'll even send you 2 wonderful surprise gifts. You can't lose!

REMEMBER: Your Free Merchandise, consisting of **2 Free Books** and **2 Free Gifts**, is worth over $20.00! No purchase is necessary, so please send for your Free Merchandise today.

Plus TWO FREE GIFTS!

We'll also send you two wonderful FREE GIFTS (worth about $10), in addition to your 2 Free Harlequin® Superromance® books!

Order online at:
www.ReaderService.com

YOUR FREE MERCHANDISE INCLUDES...

2 FREE Harlequin® Superromance® Books

AND 2 FREE Mystery Gifts

FREE MERCHANDISE VOUCHER

2 FREE BOOKS and 2 FREE GIFTS

Please send my Free Merchandise, consisting of
2 Free Books and **2 Free Mystery Gifts**.
I understand that I am under no obligation to buy
anything, as explained on the back of this card.

*About how many NEW paperback fiction books
have you purchased in the past 3 months?*

❏ 0-2   ❏ 3-6   ❏ 7 or more
E9SM   **E9SX**   **E9TA**

❏ I prefer the regular-print edition   ❏ I prefer the larger-print edition
135/336 HDL   **139/339 HDL**

Please Print

FIRST NAME

LAST NAME

ADDRESS

APT.#   CITY

STATE/PROV.   ZIP/POSTAL CODE

Offer limited to one per household and not applicable to series that subscriber is currently receiving.
Your Privacy—The Reader Service is committed to protecting your privacy. Our Privacy Policy is available online at www.ReaderService.com or upon request from the Reader Service. We make a portion of our mailing list available to reputable third parties that offer products we believe may interest you. If you prefer that we not exchange your name with third parties, or if you wish to clarify or modify your communication preferences, please visit us at www.ReaderService.com/consumerchoice.

NO PURCHASE NECESSARY!

▲ Detach card and mail today. No stamp needed. ▲

© 2010 HARLEQUIN ENTERPRISES LIMITED. ® and ™ are trademarks owned and used by the trademark owner and/or its licensee. Printed in the U.S.A.

(H-SR-12/10)

The Reader Service - Here's how it works:

Accepting your 2 free books and 2 free mystery gifts (gifts valued at approximately $10.00) places you under no obligation to buy anything. You may keep the books and gifts and return the shipping statement marked "cancel." If you do not cancel, about a month later we'll send you 6 additional books and bill you just $4.69 each for the regular-print edition or $5.44 each for the larger-print edition in the U.S. or $5.24 each for the regular-print edition or $5.99 each for the larger-print edition in Canada. That's a savings of at least 13% off the cover price. It's quite a bargain! Shipping and handling is just 50¢ per book.* You may cancel at any time, but if you choose to continue, every month we'll send you 6 more books, which you may either purchase at the discount price or return to us and cancel your subscription.

*Terms and prices subject to change without notice. Prices do not include applicable taxes. Sales tax applicable in N.Y. Canadian residents will be charged applicable taxes. Offer not valid in Quebec. All orders subject to approval. Books received may not be as shown. Credit or debit balances in a customer's account(s) may be offset by any other outstanding balance owed by or to the customer. Please allow 4 to 6 weeks for delivery. Offer available while quantities last.

▲ If offer card is missing write to: The Reader Service, P.O. Box 1867, Buffalo, NY 14240-1867 or visit www.ReaderService.com ▲

BUSINESS REPLY MAIL
FIRST-CLASS MAIL   PERMIT NO. 717   BUFFALO, NY

POSTAGE WILL BE PAID BY ADDRESSEE

THE READER SERVICE
PO BOX 1867
BUFFALO NY 14240-9952

NO POSTAGE
NECESSARY
IF MAILED
IN THE
UNITED STATES

both of those emotions from her husband and family and friends through the last long years, she couldn't fault Shawn for his feelings. Her scars were a startling sight.

Cole chose that moment to cry and both Camille and Matt turned at the interruption. "Is he fussy?" Camille asked, rushing over.

"I think he's tired. We played for a bit and he started yawning to beat the band."

"His afternoon nap was cut short today. He's probably exhausted." Camille cradled the baby in her arms and murmured soothingly to him. He quieted instantly and again Rhiannon felt a small pang.

"Go relax. I'll be down as soon as I get him to sleep."

Two hours later, Rhiannon was still thinking about Shawn as she walked down her brother's driveway to her car. No question about it, she owed him an apology for her bizarre behavior the other night—and since. And while she could probably do it in a phone call, or maybe even an email, she turned her car toward the lake. It wasn't that late and there was no time like the present. Besides, she'd probably lose her nerve if she waited too long.

She tried to figure out what to say without revealing too much of her past. She imagined Shawn apologizing for some indiscretion, a charming grin on his face and a bouquet of flowers in one hand. Or a box of candy. Or—

She turned into a local ice cream parlor, ran in and got pints of her two favorite flavors. Surely he couldn't resist a heartfelt apology and the best ice cream around.

Rhiannon tried to tell herself it was no big deal, that she was just going to stop in for a couple of minutes, deliver her apology and then head for home. But even as she had the thought, she knew it was a lie. If Shawn accepted her apology, if he invited her in, she would stay. And in doing so, open up a whole part of herself that she had buried so deep and so well that she had almost forgotten it had existed.

Still, when she got to his house she didn't linger in the car, no matter how much she wanted to. Better to just jump in with both feet and figure out how this thing was going to play out. If she spent any more time thinking about it, she would go crazy.

Making her way to the front door, she clutched the bag of ice cream in one hand and knocked with the other. He didn't immediately answer and as she stood there, a sense of overwhelming foolishness assailed her. Had she really thought he would be home? It was Saturday night and he was a young, attractive guy. He was probably out at a local bar, trying to pick up a more receptive woman.

Or maybe he had already found one, she thought with dawning horror. He could be on a date right now, or worse, in the house with the woman, having an intimate dinner that would end much better than the one he'd attempted to have with Rhiannon the week before.

She headed back toward her car at nearly a dead run. She'd almost made it when she heard Shawn's front door swing open and his very surprised, "Rhiannon?"

She turned around, more than aware of the fact that her face had gone as red as her hair—not her most becoming color, to say the least. And her first look at

Shawn had her blushing even more. He was dressed in an old pair of jeans with holes at the knees and what looked like absolutely nothing else. He was shirtless and the jeans' top button was undone, revealing only more skin where she would expect to find underwear.

And dear God, did he look good. She'd known he was well-built from the way his clothes had fit—and from the hard muscles she'd felt when he'd stood so close to her at the batting cage. But nothing had prepared her for the fact that without his shirt, Shawn was absolutely gorgeous.

His torso was long and lean, the muscles of his stomach forming a tight six pack beneath his smooth, tanned skin. A light dusting of hair started under his belly button and disappeared beneath the heavy denim of his jeans. Add in the shaggy, too-long brown hair and piercing blue eyes, the strong jaw and cut-glass cheekbones, and he was completely stunning.

And the way he was looking at her—all confused interest and tight control—was fascinating. Intriguing. Arousing. For the first time in literally years, Rhiannon found herself responding to a man. Her breath quickened as her nipples tightened beneath the heavy material of her sweater.

God, she would die of mortification if he had another woman in there, some young beautiful blonde with a perfect, unblemished body.

"What are you doing here?" He took the steps leading up to his door two at a time until he was standing only a few inches away from her.

She tried to think of something clever to say, something smart and funny and completely off-the-cuff, but she was too frazzled to do much more than stare.

"Rhiannon, are you okay?" He reached for her, but stopped himself before he actually touched her. His hand fell to his side and with it, so did the hopes Rhiannon barely allowed herself to have.

He knew. Or if he didn't, he certainly suspected. And now he would treat her just like everyone else— like a freak who could wig out at any second instead of a woman he was interested in getting to know.

Of course, could she blame him? She'd already wigged out on him, twice. It was a wonder he hadn't turned around and barred the door against her.

"I'm fine. I just stopped by to apologize. And bring you some ice cream." She held up the bag.

"Ice cream?" If possible, he looked even more puzzled.

"Yeah. Anyway, I'm sorry to bother you. I should have called first. I'll let you get back to whatever it is you were doing." She started backing toward her car.

"Hey. Hold on for a second." The weirded-out look was slowly fading, to be replaced by the sexy smile she was used to.

"Umm, sure."

"First of all, I was just working. I have a book due in a few weeks and I'm trying to get it done. Besides, I'd rather see you. And second…" His voice trailed off.

"Second?" Was that really her sounding so breathless? What had happened to the Ice Queen, the woman who had absolutely no interest in men?

"You forgot to give me the ice cream."

"Oh. Right." She handed him the bag. "Here you go."

"So, what flavors did you get?"

She stared at him blankly, shocked to realize that for

a moment, she couldn't remember what flavors she'd gotten. It would sound stupid to admit it, but the truth was her brain kind of short-circuited when he looked at her.

"Flavors, Rhiannon?" Shawn repeated. "I've found you can tell a lot about a woman by the kind of ice cream she eats."

She was intrigued despite herself, the need to flee fading in the face of his obvious pleasure in seeing her. "Really? Like what?"

"Why don't you come on in? I'll dish up a bowl and tell you all about it." His wicked grin made the invitation sound anything but innocent.

CHAPTER TWELVE

SHAWN HAD BEEN SHOCKED to find Rhiannon at his front door, but now that she was inside the house, he was really glad she'd decided to come. He'd spent the past week avoiding her as he tried to figure out just what he could take—and what he couldn't—and he'd missed her. Probably more than he should have. It had been a very pleasant surprise to find her on his doorstep, bearing ice cream and acting delightfully nervous.

Was it wrong of him to enjoy the fact that he made her nervous? he wondered as he pulled out two bowls and an ice cream scoop. Probably, but since she didn't seem to be afraid—only aware of him on a whole new level—he wasn't going to beat himself up over it.

She was dressed in a long-sleeved pink sweater and a pair of jeans that lovingly hugged her slight curves, and not for the first time, he realized that she was too thin. How long had she been suffering? he wondered. How long had she been wasting away because of something some monster had done to her?

He'd spent hours on the internet in the past few days, trying to ferret out what had happened to her, but nothing new had turned up since that first day. The not knowing what had happened to her was eating him up inside. Driving him crazy. The idea that someone had hurt her upset him more than anything had in a very long time—maybe ever.

"So, tell me about this theory you have about ice cream flavors," Rhiannon said as she settled onto the same barstool she'd occupied the last time she'd been there.

"What kind did you get?" he asked, reaching into the bag to pull out one of the containers.

"Uh-uh. That's not fair. You have to tell me your theory and then we'll see if you're right."

Her voice was low and teasing and he felt himself hardening in response. Her nervousness was still there, but it was countered with a sultriness that had him thinking of hot sex and endless nights in bed. He knew he was rushing things in his head—she was too skittish for either of those things just yet—but that didn't stop his fantasies any more than it stopped the need rushing through him.

Part of him wanted nothing more than to cross over to her, pull her into his arms and kiss her. But he was interested enough in her to put on the brakes, to take things as slowly as Rhiannon needed him to. In the meantime, he would content himself with remembering what her body had felt like against his, what she had tasted like as his mouth had explored hers.

"Well, I've found that there are three types of ice cream—and a certain type of woman enjoys each kind."

"Do tell." She leaned back on the stool, arching a brow in that way he loved.

"The first kind is the one who loves pure flavors, ice cream with nothing added to it like vanilla or chocolate, strawberry or mango."

"And what type of woman likes that kind of ice cream?"

He stared hard at the bag for a second, trying hard to figure out what kind of ice cream Rhiannon had brought him. He would really hate to insult her—or worse, send her running again—by saying the wrong thing.

"One who knows her own mind. She's straight-forward and uncluttered, speaks her mind and isn't afraid of a challenge. She's smart and very often what you see with her is what you get."

Rhiannon watched him carefully. "That kind of person sounds a little boring to me."

"I don't think so. There's something kind of refresh-ing about always knowing where you stand with her. I like women who know their own mind and aren't afraid to go after it."

"I bet. And the second type of woman?"

"Oh, she's the kind who likes things a little more variety, whether it's ice cream or relationships. But who is so used to denying herself that she doesn't understand that low-fat frozen yogurt or sugar-free ice cream really isn't ice cream at all—just a poor substitute."

"And this woman is into denial? You don't think that's complicated?"

He grinned. "I didn't say she was uncomplicated. But I'm pretty sure I can handle her."

"You think so, huh?"

"I'm feeling relatively confident." He reached for the bag a second time, but she stopped him.

"You haven't finished your analysis quite yet."

"Wouldn't you rather eat ice cream?"

"Not even close. I'm spellbound."

"All right then. The third type likes the everything-but-the-kitchen sink variety of ice cream. You know, triple chocolate chunk with pecans and caramel. Or peanut butter and fudge brownie with strawberry sauce."

"Peanut butter and fudge brownie? With strawberry?" Rhiannon shuddered. "That sounds revolting."

"You know what I mean."

"I guess." She looked doubtful, but finally asked, "And what fascinating personality quirks does the kitchen-sink woman have?"

"She's the woman who takes a long time to make up her mind, the one who doesn't know exactly what she wants until she tries it on for size. She's a little wild, not quick to be pinned down. An adventurer."

"Sounds like she's a little over the top."

"Maybe a little."

"But you can handle her, too, right?" Rhiannon's eyes were laughing at him and as he watched her he realized it was the first time since they'd met that she seemed truly happy. Completely relaxed.

"I don't know about that—she might be a bit much for me." He glanced at the bag she was still guarding. "Can I dish up the ice cream now?"

"If you think you can take it."

"I'm pretty tough."

She laughed. "For a guy who spends all day playing with superheroes, I'm sure you're very tough."

"Hey, Shadeslayer's a complicated guy. He keeps me on my toes." He reached into the bag, absolutely certain that he was going to be pulling out vanilla or strawberry or their equivalent. What he got, however, was a tub of Turtle Brownie Fudge ice cream followed by one of Triple Berry Cheesecake.

Surprised, he glanced up to find Rhiannon watching him with a smirk. "So, what do you think of your Ice Cream Woman analysis now?"

He thought he was a much luckier man than he'd originally suspected. "It's never wrong, so I'm guessing there's a whole side of you I haven't seen yet."

"Never wrong, huh? You've done some kind of scientific study on this?"

"I wouldn't *exactly* call it scientific."

"So what would you call it?"

He shifted, tried to think of a nice way to put it. Finally, he said, "I've eaten ice cream with a lot of women in my life."

She snorted. "I just bet you have."

He scooped a couple of scoops of ice cream into each bowl, then grabbed them and headed into the family room. "Come on—it's more comfortable in here."

"I'll say. It's downright hedonistic."

He watched as she sank into one corner of his huge sofa, curling her legs up underneath her as she started in on her ice cream.

Shawn watched her for a few seconds, unable to look away. He liked seeing her here, in his favorite room. Liked having her here, curled up on his sofa, enjoying her treat with a sensual abandon that had him close to exploding with need.

But it was more than how sexy she was, more than the fact that she kept him on his toes. Despite their rocky start—or rather, starts—he liked her. Really liked her. She was smart, capable, resilient and, despite everything, strong enough to stand against him when she needed to.

She was also fragile, and he found himself wanting to wrap her up, to keep her safe from whoever it was that had hurt her, from whatever it was that haunted her.

He was still a little skittish, still a little concerned with how much time he spent thinking about Rhiannon. How much time he spent trying to come up with a way to be with her. And even worse, a way to fix her. If he wasn't careful, he was going to end up falling for her, seriously, and anyone who knew him knew he didn't do serious. He wasn't about to start now, no matter how much Rhiannon interested him.

Even so, he did his best to ignore the alarm his subconscious was sounding. Just because he found her fascinating didn't mean he was going to end up falling in love with her. He didn't do love, and even if he had wanted to try a real relationship on for size, it wouldn't be with a woman as emotionally devastated as Rhiannon. Cynthia had more than cured him of his need to play white knight years ago.

Uncomfortable with the direction his thoughts were taking, Shawn went over to the stereo in the corner and turned it on. Immediately the Dave Matthews Band filled the room between them.

"I love this song," Rhiannon said as the opening chords of "Crash Into Me" came through the speakers.

"I do, too. I saw them live when they came through Dallas a few months ago—it was a really good time."

"I bet. I planned on going to that show, but something came up. I missed a good one, huh?"

"It was awesome."

He launched into a description of the concert, which led to a discussion of other concerts they had both attended. Before he knew it, an hour had passed and both of their bowls were empty.

"Do you want some more ice cream?" he asked Rhiannon, who looked down at her empty bowl in surprise.

"How do you do that?" she demanded. "I usually have trouble eating, but when I'm with you I can't seem to get enough food."

"I like watching you eat." He reached for her bowl. "Can I get you another scoop?"

"No way! I'm probably one step away from a sugar coma as we speak."

"But what a way to go."

"No doubt. I'll take chocolate, caramel and pecans any way I can get them. My brother used to tease me that I would eat Turtles out of a dirty shoe as long as I could get my caramel fix." She glanced down at her watch. "I should probably get going."

"Why? Do you turn into a pumpkin at 9:30 p.m.?"

She looked surprised. "I thought you did. I'm noticing a distinctly orange cast to your skin and wanted to leave before it got any more embarrassing for you."

He burst out laughing, and that's when he had the first inkling that he just might be in trouble. But how was he supposed to keep from falling for her, when that deadpan sense of humor of hers kept sneaking up on him at the oddest times?

"I really like you, Rhiannon." The words were out before he'd known he was going to say them, but as they stretched between them he felt no desire to take them back.

The smile faded from her face. "Don't."

He scooted over on the couch, until their knees were just touching. "Why not?"

"I'm a mess, in case you hadn't noticed. Definitely not good relationship material."

Well, he certainly wouldn't be able to say she hadn't warned him. Of course, he'd already figured out the mess part for himself. Yet, as he looked at her in the rosy glow cast by the end-table lamp, he felt no urge to back away. The warning bells had gone silent, and while he didn't know if that was a good thing or a bad one, he had the feeling he was about to find out.

"So what are you doing here, then? You could have just kept sending me those boring emails of yours."

"Those emails are efficient."

"Those emails are insane. If they were any more impersonal, I would think they'd come from the Internal Revenue Service."

"Ouch. Nothing quite like being compared to the IRS to cut a girl down to size."

"You never answered my question."

"No, I didn't." She looked down at the bowl in her lap and all that luscious hair of hers fell over her face like a curtain.

"Hey." He reached forward, took the bowl from her nervous hands and set it on the coffee table. "I can't see your face."

"Is that such a tragedy?" She didn't look up.

"It is when I'm trying to get a straight answer from you." He cupped her chin between his thumb and index finger and tilted her head up, so that she had no choice but to look him in the eye.

What he saw in hers had his breath lodging in his chest. He didn't know how to describe it, didn't even know if there was a name for the look she gave him. All he knew was that the last time he'd felt like this, it had been after he'd crashed his motorcycle and hit the pavement so hard that every ounce of oxygen had been expelled from his lungs.

"So," he murmured, his lips brushing across her forehead and down her cheek. "If you're such a mess, why did you come here tonight?"

She tilted her head to the side, and he kissed his way down her temple to her cheek, down her cheek to the corner of her mouth. "You're going to make me say it, aren't you?"

"Say what?" He nibbled along her jaw, reveling in the sudden catch in her breathing, the slight trembling of her body beneath his.

"I came here tonight because I like you, too. God knows, it'll probably end up being a train wreck—"

His mouth closed over hers, effectively cutting off the doom-and-gloom message she seemed so intent on delivering.

CHAPTER THIRTEEN

RHIANNON DRESSED nervously for her date with Shawn. It was stupid, she knew, to get herself this worked up, especially considering the fact that they'd spent the better part of their free time for the past week and a half together.

But tonight was different—or at least, it felt different. Tonight wasn't about hanging out at his house in comfy jeans and sweaters. It wasn't about playing pinball and video games and gorging themselves on pizza any more than it was about him coming to her office where she drove him crazy trying to pin him down about specifics for his party.

No, tonight was their first grown-up date—no bats or batting cages allowed. He was taking her to Mr. D's, one of the fanciest piano bars and restaurants in Austin.

She'd dressed carefully, switching outfits more times than she cared to admit—even to herself. The one she'd finally settled on was pretty good, if she did say so herself, even if it didn't show any skin.

For a moment, she thought longingly of the closet full of short, flirty dresses she'd owned in what seemed like another life. Dresses that had celebrated her body instead of covered it up, that made her feel young and vibrant instead of matronly and boring.

Of course, the fact that she was dating a twenty-nine-year-old probably didn't help the fact that she suddenly felt every one of her forty years. Shawn was so handsome, so fun-loving, so young that sometimes she felt like a wet blanket next to him.

He never treated her like that, though, never made her feel like she was anything less than an interesting, attractive woman. But sometimes she couldn't help wondering what Shawn thought of her. How he saw her, in her pantsuits and turtlenecks, with her long hair and scars.

For the first time in a long time, it mattered to her what a man thought of her appearance. It was a strange feeling, this wanting to be sexy for a man after years of wanting nothing more than to blend in to the wallpaper. Even now, as she wore the only fancy set of underwear she owned—one she'd bought on impulse that afternoon as a sort of birthday gift to herself—she wondered what it meant.

Was she ready for sex with Shawn? Hell, was she ready for sex period? She'd only had sex with two men in her life, the first one a college boyfriend and the second one her husband of almost fifteen years—which meant that it had been well over seventeen years since she'd been with anyone but Richard. Even worse, it had been nearly three years since she'd had sex at all.

Oh, she and Richard had tried to make love after the attack, but each time had been an unmitigated disaster worse than the one before it. At first Richard had been understanding, but as months had passed and she'd remained unable to respond to him, he'd grown more and more impatient. One of his parting shots had been that he couldn't stand living with a woman who recoiled every time he so much as looked at her.

She hadn't blamed him—or at least, she hadn't blamed him much. After all, they'd had a good, active sex life all the way up to the attack—was it any wonder Richard had grown frustrated at his wife's lack of interest in him?

Understanding only went so far.

And now, here she was, thinking of opening herself up to a man all over again. Of opening herself up to *Shawn,* who didn't have the history Richard had had with her. Who didn't know what her body had looked like when it had been young and unscarred.

What would he think of how she looked? she wondered, as she slipped a pair of sparkly earring into her ears. He'd told her to wear something pretty, something sexy, and though she'd done her best, she knew she was a far cry from the twentysomethings he was used to, with their firm, unblemished skin and their ability to have sex with him without spending hours upon hours psyching themselves up to do the deed.

But he hadn't asked any of the twentysomethings out to dinner, she reminded herself fiercely. He'd asked *her* out, had spent the past week and a half seeking out *her* company.

Surely that had to count for something. She just wished she knew how much.

A knock at the front door interrupted her self-reflection and panic spurted through her. She wasn't ready for this, wasn't sure she could take this step. Was afraid tonight would be yet another disaster. No matter how much she told herself it didn't matter, deep inside her she knew that it did. Not just because she was forty today and the fact that she was unable to be intimate with a man was starting to really bother her, but also because she didn't want to mess things up with Shawn. No matter how much she told herself they were just having fun, just hanging out, just keeping things casual, she knew that she was lying to herself. She was falling for Shawn in a big way, and the idea that this might be their last date—that she might screw things up so bad this time that there would be no more chances—haunted her.

Closing her eyes for a brief moment, she took a deep breath. Tried to relax. Did her best to center herself despite the riot of emotions spinning around inside of her. Then with a quick prayer that the night wouldn't be a complete and total debacle, she went to let him in.

THE SECOND RHIANNON opened the door, Shawn knew he was in trouble. And not just a little trouble like he'd originally feared, but trouble of the huge, irrevocable, inescapable variety. He'd been waiting for this moment all day, had spent more time thinking about her than he had Shadeslayer, and that was something that had never happened to him with another woman—particularly when he had a deadline fast approaching. But it had happened to him twice now with Rhiannon, and like the first time, she hadn't disappointed him.

She looked beautiful, all that crazy, techno-colored hair of hers falling straight and gleaming nearly to her waist. Unable to resist, he reached out and touched it, making sure he moved cautiously so as not to startle Rhiannon—the past ten days had taught him that she would grant him all kinds of liberties as long as he moved slowly as he took them.

It felt as good as it looked—all cool, silky-smoothness. He wrapped a few strands around his fingers, relishing the way all the colors stood out against his skin. He wanted to raise it to his lips, to feel it slide over him like it did every night in his dreams.

His body hardened painfully at the reminder of how many nights he'd woken up in a cold sweat, his body aching from dreams of having all that cool silkiness wrapped around him while he made love to Rhiannon.

Pulling his gaze away from her hair, he looked into her bittersweet chocolate eyes and the uncertainty there made him both sad and angry. When she forgot to be self-conscious, Rhiannon was one of the most amazing women he'd ever met and he couldn't help wondering what she'd been like before whatever had happened had damaged her so severely. The fact that she didn't see how great she was—that someone had hurt her so bad that she was almost blind to her own worth—made him angrier than anything ever had. Angrier even than he'd been as he'd watched depression eat away at Cynthia until there was nothing left of her.

Knowing his anger wasn't what she needed to see right now, he shoved it down deep inside of himself, then smiled lazily at her. "Hey, there."

"Hey." Her answering smile didn't quite touch her eyes.

"You look absolutely gorgeous." She'd chosen a long-sleeved jumpsuit the color of dark, ripe cherries. While it covered most of her body—and wasn't that a shame—it was made of a soft, clingy material that molded to every one of her mouth-watering curves. In the past couple of weeks, she'd been eating better and had put on a few pounds that had nicely rounded out her slender frame, pounds that her outfit showed off to their best advantage.

Add in the sexy, black stiletto sandals on her feet— along with the pretty silver toe rings—and it was all he could do to keep from barreling into her apartment, locking the door and having his wicked way with her.

"Thank you."

"I'm serious. You should wear that color all the time. You look amazing in it."

At his compliment, her cheeks turned the color of the pomegranates he devoured by the bucketful in the summertime, and he wanted nothing more than to pull her into his arms and kiss every part of her.

Patience, he reminded himself, even as he shoved his hands in his pockets as a precaution. Eventually he'd be able to make love to her, be able to hold her in his arms as he explored every part of her. He just had to be patient—even if it killed him.

"You look wonderful, too."

"Thanks. Are you ready to go?"

"Sure. Just let me get my purse."

They drove to the restaurant in companionable silence, broken by spurts of conversation that he could barely hold his own in. A couple of times Rhiannon sent him strange looks, but it wasn't like he could help himself. She smelled so good, the honeysuckle scent he loved so much was magnified in the close confines of the car until he could barely keep his eyes—and his hands—off of her. The idea of waiting much longer to have her was agony, but the last thing he wanted to do was spook her.

By the time they were seated in a big, comfortable booth against the back wall of the piano bar, he could barely keep his impatience to touch her in check. As soon as the waiter had taken their drink and appetizer order, he reached across the table for her hand, being careful to ask permission with a look before he actually took hold of it.

She'd gotten better about letting him touch her, but she was still edgy and he understood that, tried to account for it no matter how worked up she got him.

"Dance with me," he murmured.

"What, now?" she asked, eyes wide. "We just got here."

"I want to hold you."

She smiled, a soft, sweet curve of her lips that made her look even more beautiful—and terribly vulnerable. Reminding himself of how delicate she was, Shawn pulled her to her feet and onto the intimate dance floor. And as his arms closed around her, bringing her long, slender body flush against his own, he closed his eyes and simply breathed her in. Then, they began to dance.

THE SONG WAS A LONG, trembling sigh. A whisper and a plea. A promise made, then broken.

Rhiannon listened to the lonely call of a solo saxophone as it was joined by the slow throb of the drums and the tinkling rhythm of the black and white piano keys. It called to her, opened her up, made her remember what it was like to want. What it was like to need.

Shawn's right hand was on her waist, his fingers

resting against the curve of her side while his left hand
cradled her right. Heat emanated from him, working its
way through her until he was all she could feel. All she
could see or smell or hear as he moved them smoothly
across the dance floor.

She knew they weren't the only ones on the floor,
had seen four or five other couples when she had
allowed Shawn to pull her from the booth. But she
couldn't have said where they were in relation to her
and Shawn, any more than she could have described
what they looked like. In those long, intimate moments
when Shawn held her in his arms, all she knew was
him.

The songs changed, going from a throb to a wail and
back again, and still they danced. Shawn's hand slid
from her waist to her hip to the curve of her bottom and
she never said a word, never felt a twinge of the anxiety
that normally came when a man got too close. Instead,
she simply relaxed and enjoyed the sensations coursing
through her. It had been so long since she'd felt them
that they were almost foreign, nearly inexplicable, and
she remembered, for a moment, what it was like to be
seventeen and feeling the sweet ache of desire for the
very first time.

And then even that memory faded away under the
pleasure that came with being able to hold Shawn, to be
held by him, without fear. She never wanted the music
to end.

But eventually it did, and as the band took a break,
Shawn escorted her back to their table. The pomegran-
ate martini she had ordered was sitting there, along
with his scotch and the crab-cake appetizer they'd ordered to share.

"You're a good dancer," she said, as she lifted her drink to her mouth. The tangy sweetness of the martini hit her tongue and she marveled at how good it tasted. But then again, everything tasted good when she was with Shawn. After three years of food turning to sawdust in her mouth, it was a welcome surprise—and pleasure.

"Didn't step on your foot once. Which is a good thing, considering the shoes you're wearing."

"You noticed my shoes?" she asked, surprised.

"Seeing as how they're the sexiest sandals I think I've ever seen in my life, yeah, you could say I noticed them."

She couldn't stop the grin from spreading across her face. Shawn had called her shoes sexy. Admittedly, it wasn't he same as if he'd actually called her sexy, but still. She wasn't a total loser in the attraction department, it seemed—despite her inability to show off her body as so many of the other women in the room were doing.

"Thank you for bringing me here. I'm having a great time."

"I'm glad." Shawn reached across the table for her hand, squeezed it then brought it to his lips where he planted a lingering kiss on her palm. His thumb stroked over the back of her hand and he smiled. "I love how soft your hands are. Is your skin like this all over?"

She felt herself freeze at the question, her entire body turning to stone as she thought of the scars that criss-crossed so much of her body. They were thin, yes, but slick and slightly bumpy and they felt nothing like the skin of her hands, which she babied. They were one

of the few parts of her body he hadn't touched and she
admitted to being more than a little vain about them.

Shawn didn't seem to notice her reaction or, if he
did, he never said anything. Gradually, she found herself relaxing again, refusing to let anything ruin the
wonderful evening Shawn had planned for them.

Dinner was delicious, though she couldn't have said
what she ordered—only that she once again cleaned
her plate. So caught up in conversation with Shawn,
she hadn't paid any attention to what she was eating
until the only thing left on her plate was the sauce and
edible garnish. When she found herself studying the
flowers, wondering if they were any good, she decided
it was way past time to put her fork down.

"What do you want for dessert?" Shawn asked as the
waiter cleared their plates away. "They have a molten
chocolate cake here that's fabulous."

"Are you kidding? I'm stuffed."

"Aw, come on, we'll split one. You have to try it."

She started to protest, but in the end gave in—because it was easier and because the idea of sharing
something with Shawn, even something as simple as
dessert, was too delicious a prospect to pass up.

But when the waiter brought the small, round cake
a few minutes later, she realized with chagrin that it
had a lit birthday candle in it. The band launched into
a rousing rendition of "Happy Birthday" that many of
the waiters—and patrons—joined in on. Her cheeks
burned as she blew out the candle and when they were
no longer the focus of half the eyes in the place, she
hissed, "I can't believe you did that!"

"Hey, a fortieth birthday is nothing to sneeze at. You
deserved to celebrate in style."

Some of her pleasure in the evening dimmed as she realized that he hadn't set up this fabulous night just because, but to celebrate a birthday she was more than happy to let pass unheralded. But she was being stupid—it didn't matter why he'd arranged the date. The important thing was that he had.

"How did you know it was my birthday? I know I didn't tell you."

"Logan let the cat out of the bag. But that begs the question, why didn't you tell me? Isn't that the kind of thing a guy should know about the woman he's dating?"

"Is that what we're doing?" she asked curiously. "Dating?"

"Well, we sure as hell aren't playing tiddlywinks," he answered impatiently. "I certainly thought we were dating. And you're dodging the question again."

"I don't know. I guess I wasn't too keen on pointing out the fact that I am now eleven years older than you."

"Ten and a half, and who really cares?"

"Are you saying that even after all these weeks you don't care? At all?"

"Of course I don't. I care even less now than I did when I first asked you out, and you know I didn't care then. Why would that change?" He looked puzzled, and a little hurt. "Unless it's changed for you?"

"It hasn't, but—" She paused, tried to figure out how to get across what she wanted to say.

"But what?

"I think it must be easier not to care if you're the younger partner in the pair. I mean, my ex-husband

was six years older than I was and I never even thought
about it. But now that I'm so much older than you—"

"Ten years is not that big a deal."

"Ten and a half. And it's more than a decade, Shawn.
That is a big deal."

"Only if you let it be." His eyes burned with an intensity that cut through the darkness of the restaurant.
"Do you enjoy being with me?"

"Of course I do."

"And do we have things in common? Do you like
talking to me?"

"You know I do."

"Then come on, Rhiannon. Don't you think we've
both got more important things to worry about than
whose birth certificate is older?"

Intellectually, she knew he was right. If they were
both happy, what did it matter which one of them was
born first? But emotionally, it wasn't that easy—maybe
because she knew she came with a whole lot more baggage attached than Shawn did. Her age was just one
more suitcase in a pile that was threateningly large.

She didn't say that, though, she couldn't. Because
to do so would be to open up the door for a whole
bunch of questions she didn't feel anywhere close to
being ready to answer. So she just smiled and nodded.
"You're right. It doesn't matter."

He studied her for a minute, as if testing the sincerity
of her words. He didn't look convinced, but in the end
he let it drop, too—maybe because he didn't want to
ruin her birthday.

Or maybe, the more cynical side of her nature said,
because he'd already used all his best arguments.

"I got you something," he said, before reaching into his jacket pocket and pulling out a long, flat box.

"You didn't have to do that—"

"I wanted to."

"Still, jewelry is—"

"Always a man's prerogative to buy for the woman he cares about." He slid the box across the table. "Now, quit arguing and open the thing. I've been waiting all night to give it to you."

Because it had been too long since a man had given her jewelry and because she was dying to see what Shawn had chosen for her, Rhiannon did as he said. Then gasped as she stared at the intricate gold charm bracelet that sparkled against the black velvet of the box.

The bracelet itself was a series of beveled links, and hanging from it were two finely wrought charms—one of a party hat, its polka dots made up of small, semi-precious stones and another of an ice cream cone with a perfect, ruby cherry on top.

Her throat clogged as she stared at it, shocked at how much thought had gone into the present. Surely a man who was just in a relationship for a little fun wouldn't spend so much time coming up with the perfect gift.

"Ice cream, huh?" she asked, as she held the bracelet up to the light and admired it. "Where'd you find a charm like that?"

"I have my ways." The look he gave her was surprisingly serious considering the fact that she was obviously thrilled with his gift. "I wanted to give you happy memories for your birthday, a reminder of good times to take away from the darkness of whatever it is in your past that you can't talk about. We can add to it as new memories creep up, until there's nothing left of the bad ones to hurt you."

Tears welled in her eyes, and when she wanted to talk, there was a giant lump in her throat, one that no amount of throat clearing was going to get rid of.

How could he have done this for her, without even knowing what bad memories she was running from? How could he have known, instinctively, that this was what she needed—a tangible reminder of everything good in her life—when she hadn't had a clue herself?

How could he have known her that well?

She was still asking herself that question when Shawn dropped her back at her condo a little over an hour later. "Do you want to come in?" she asked as she fumbled for her keys. "I can make some coffee—"

"If I come in, it won't be for coffee, Rhiannon."

The keys hit the ground with a thud. "Oh, right. Okay."

He bent down and retrieved them, found the key to her front door and slowly inserted it in her lock. A second later, he had opened her front door, though he made no move to cross the threshold.

"So, do you want to come in?" she asked again, holding her breath as she did so, knowing the invitation she was extending and only hoping she could follow through on it.

His eyes blazed and she swore she could see every one of his muscles tighten. He searched her face for long seconds, and though she didn't know what he was looking for, she tried her best to give it to him—even as the voice in the back of her head came back with a vengeance.

What are you doing? it screamed. *You aren't ready*

for this—not even close. You're going to end up making a fool of yourself all over again.

Part of her struggle must have shown in her face, because Shawn sighed, one second before the tension melted from his muscles. "I think I'll pass tonight."

"Why? Don't you want to—"

"I want to very much." He reached for her, letting his hands settle softly around her waist. When she didn't move away, he pulled her toward him slowly until she was fully in his arms, held so tightly against him that she could feel the rapid beating of his heart and the burning hardness of the erection he didn't even try to hide. "But, as I said before, I'm in no rush. I can wait until you're ready."

"Shawn, it's okay. Really. You gave me such a lovely birthday—"

His eyes cooled considerably. "I'm glad you enjoyed it. But I'm not in the habit of making the women I take out pay me back in sexual favors."

"I didn't mean it like that."

"I know. But when I finally make love to you, Rhiannon Jenkins, you're going to do a hell of a lot more than grit your teeth and bear it." He lowered his mouth to within an inch of hers. "Now kiss me, so I can get out of here before I change my mind."

His lips were firm and cool against hers and still her head spun dizzily.

"What would it take to change your mind?" she asked as he let her go reluctantly.

"The desire in your eyes outweighing the fear." He kissed her again, briefly, then took the steps back to the street, two at a time.

"What if that never happens?" she called after him, no longer the least bit surprised at his perception.

"Oh, it'll happen," he answered.

"How do you know?"

"Because if it doesn't, we both just might die of sexual frustration."

CHAPTER FOURTEEN

"I GOT MY INVITATION yesterday," Robert said as he swooped around Shawn and slam-dunked the basketball. "Classy."

Shawn rebounded, then took the ball up the court. His best friend started crowding him, his big body making it nearly impossible to get a shot off.

"I know," Shawn grunted, doing some fancy footwork in an effort to evade him. "Rhiannon's doing a fabulous job with the whole thing. It's great—all I have to do is point to a few things on a sheet of paper and then show up the night of the party. I should have thought of this party planner thing a long time ago."

"Yeah, because in the past it was so hard to buy a six-pack and open a bag of tortilla chips."

Shawn ignored him as he set up for a basket, let it sail and then watched in frustration as Robert popped up and caught the ball seconds before it sailed through the hoop. A quick run down the court with Shawn on his heels and Robert slam dunked the thing again.

"You know, I'm beginning to think we need to try a new game," Shawn panted as he ran the ball back up the court for what felt like the millionth time.

"Why? I like this one."

"Well, of course you do. You're built like a damn

mountain." He feinted left, went right and finally sent the ball soaring into the basket for three points.

"Listen to you whining." Robert was up the court in a flash, moving fast for such a big man. "Careful, Shawn, you might break a nail."

Shawn flipped him off, then positioned himself under the basket, bracing for impact. Robert might be tall and big, but he was also pretty much a one-trick pony—with his size, he'd never had to be anything else. Sure enough, he barreled up to the basket, jumped and prepared to dunk the ball just as Shawn shot his hand up and sent the ball flying wildly down the court.

They scrambled after it and spent the next few minutes trash-talking each other companionably, before Robert finally called a halt.

"All right, all right. Time for a beer."

"What, you getting old or something, man?"

"Or something. I was up all night and I'm tired."

"Problems at work?" Shawn grabbed the ball and they started the short walk back to his house from the park.

Robert's grin was sly. "Not exactly. It was more of a personal thing."

Shawn started to ask more when Robert's meaning hit him. "Lucky bastard."

"Damn straight. Lissa's the best thing that ever happened to me. You should get yourself a real woman, Shawn, instead of those good-time girls you usually date."

When Shawn didn't answer with his usual volley of insults, Robert's eyes narrowed speculatively. "Or have you already found one?"

"Don't go picking out wedding venues just yet,

Mom," he joked as they let themselves into his house. "It's just a casual thing that's gotten slightly out of hand."

They cruised into the family room, where he grabbed two beers from the bar fridge and tossed one to Robert. Why hadn't he made some joke about dating and simply moved past it? he wondered as he twisted off the bottle cap and took a long gulp of his beer. Robert was like a bloodhound—once he was on the scent of a story, it was almost impossible to get him off.

Sure enough, his best friend started in the second they were both sprawled on the couch, a baseball game blaring on the TV.

"So, who is this woman who has you thinking about settling down?"

The familiar discomfort assailed Shawn at his words. "I never said anything about settling down."

"Yeah. But you didn't break out in hives, either, at the mere mention of the *R* word. I figure that's a hell of an improvement in a short time, so some woman must be responsible."

"The *R* word?" Shawn asked incredulously. "What the hell is that?"

"You know. *Relationship.*"

"What are we, twelve? The *R* word? Really?"

"I didn't want to spook you. As mentioned above, you get freaked out when that word comes up in conversations."

"It's not that I don't want a relationship, it's just…"

"That you don't want a relationship. I get it. Cynthia did a number on you and you've been carrying that guilt around for years. Don't you think it's time you let it go and tried to be happy?"

"I am happy."

Robert snorted. "You're unentangled. That's not the same thing."

"It sure looks the same from over here."

"Yeah, well, it's not. Consider the fact that the two longest—and most important—relationships in your life are with me and your agent. What does that tell you?"

"That I'm selective." He eyed Robert balefully. "Oh, right, that can't be true. I *am* friends with you."

It was Robert's turn to flip him off. "Go ahead and make fun, but you know I'm right. This Peter Pan complex of yours is getting a little old."

He choked on his beer, nearly spewed it across the room. "Peter Pan complex? What the hell? I don't wear green tights and fly around Never Never Land."

"You might as well. Ever since Cynthia died, you spend your days running from yourself. Running from commitment, responsibility, emotion. Don't you think it's time you moved on?"

"You act like I'm wearing a hair shirt and flogging myself twice a day. My life is great." Shawn held his arms out wide, gestured to the room they were sitting in.

"Of course it is. Why wouldn't it be—it's completely superficial."

A drop of sweat rolled down Shawn's back and he sprang to his feet, not sure how to respond to Robert's sudden attack. It wasn't like his friend to go on like this, to push him against a wall. He didn't like it.

"Let me ask you something. When's the last time

you connected with a woman? Really connected, I mean?"

Rhiannon's face rose, unbidden, before him and the cold sweat moved from his back to his entire body.

"Last night, actually." He crossed to the fridge, grabbed another beer.

"I'm not talking about sex."

"Neither am I!" He started to pace. "You act like I'm some kind of Lothario who uses women and then throws them away. I don't do that."

"No, but you don't let them get close to you, either."

"You know what?" he asked, eyeing Robert with ill-disguised hostility. "I think I liked you better before you got married and started a family. This whole psychoanalyzing thing is a bit much."

"Sorry." Robert held his hand up, as if calling a truce. "Look, I'll back off. It's just, Rhiannon's different than the other women you date. I like her and so does Lissa—I don't want to see you hurt her, even accidentally."

"I never said I was dating Rhiannon."

"No, but you've talked about her more in the past two weeks than all the other women you've dated in the past two years combined. It's not rocket science."

"So why'd you ask who I was dating if you already knew?"

Robert shrugged. "To see if you'd fess up."

"Look, it's no big deal. We're taking things slow, just seeing where they're going to end up."

"Slow, huh? I didn't know that word was in your vocabulary."

"Give me a break, will you? I'm still trying to figure things out myself."

"Sure." Robert turned toward the television. "Take all the time you need."

"Gee, thanks."

Shawn spent the rest of the day trying to ignore Robert's words and pretend that his friend didn't have a point. But the problem was, he knew he did.

He had run from commitment ever since Cynthia, had refused to get close to any woman in case she died. And emotionally fragile women, forget it. Cynthia—with her dark moods and rages and depressive funks—had been more than enough for one lifetime.

Yet, here he was again on the brink of something serious with Rhiannon. He might have downplayed it for Robert, but he knew very well that his feelings for Rhiannon were growing, evolving. Becoming more dangerous. It was a little disconcerting, as if the ground was shifting beneath his feet after years of remaining steady. He wasn't quite sure what to do with it.

Because if spending time with her for the past three weeks had taught him anything, it was that his first instincts had been right on—she was incredibly delicate, incredibly damaged, and he didn't want to be the man to break her any more than she was already broken.

Last night, when she'd invited him into her apartment, it had taken every ounce of willpower he had not to jump all over the invitation she'd issued—and her. He wanted her so badly, wanted to feel her moving beneath him as he sank into her, that restraining those feelings was torture.

On that, at least, Robert had been dead-on. Shawn wasn't used to denying himself, wasn't used to waiting for what he wanted. For years, he had gone after whatever had caught his eye—in work and in personal relationships—and had usually wrapped it up in short order.

But Rhiannon was different. *He* was different when he was with her. Though most nights he was so frustrated he thought he would blow a gasket, for the first time in a very long time he was simply enjoying *being* with a woman. Enjoying holding her and kissing her and talking to her without always expecting more.

Did that mean he was serious about her? He didn't know. All he knew was that she meant more to him than anyone had in a very long time and that he would wait for her as long as it took.

He'd spent the past six years convinced he didn't have anything real left to give, certain that his ability to trust and love and commit had dried up the day he'd walked into the apartment he shared with Cynthia and found her hanging from the beam that ran straight down the center of their living room.

He had loved her, had spent two years helping her battle the bipolar disorder that had made her a whirling dervish one minute and unable to crawl out of bed the next. But nothing he'd done had made any difference, and in the end, his love hadn't been enough to keep her alive.

So he'd taken himself out of the game and it had worked fine for him for a long time. The fact that he was now back in the game—back where he'd started so many years before—caring about a woman who was far too fragile was scary as hell.

But he couldn't seem to stop himself. There was something about Rhiannon that got to him, that made him feel more than he'd ever planned on. Too bad he had no idea what to do with those feelings, now that he had them.

"SO HOW ARE THINGS GOING with that handsome graphic-artist guy you told me about a few weeks ago?" Camille asked as she painted her toes an oddly becoming shade of blue. Rhiannon stared at them, bemused, as she tried to reconcile the brother she knew with the man who had married a blue-nailed artist with purple streaks in her hair and multiple tattoos. If she hadn't seen, personally, how happy they were together, she would never have believed it.

Rhiannon shrugged. "They're going fine."

"Just fine? Hey, you aren't going to paint your toes that color, are you?"

"Why wouldn't I?" Rhiannon responded. "It's the same color I always use." Still, she hesitated to open the bottle. It looked so boring next to Camille's periwinkle-blue polish.

"I know, I know. But why don't you shake things up, wear a color a little sexier? I can tell you on great authority that men like a woman with fancy toes."

"Really?" Rhiannon shot her an arch look. "And dare I ask how exactly you know this?"

Her sister-in-law laughed. It was the low, throaty sound of a woman who knew exactly how much her husband desired her and again, a squeeze of envy tightened Rhiannon's stomach. What she wouldn't give for Camille's easy sexuality and her certainty that the man in her life loved her. Most days, Rhiannon couldn't be certain that Shawn even desired her.

Oh, he complimented her regularly, held her and

kissed her, but he never tried for more—even when she let him know she was receptive. His words echoed in her head regularly, about taking her when her desire outweighed her fear, but despite the fact that they'd seen each other almost every day for the past two weeks, he'd made no move to make good on that promise.

"Come on," Camille cajoled. "Live a little, Rhiannon. Cutting loose every once in a while is good for you."

"You really think the blue polish will look good on me?" she asked, dropping the familiar old peach one back in her purse. She felt a mild twinge, as if she was saying goodbye to yet another old friend. But she didn't change her mind—she'd decided more than once in the past few weeks that she was tired of being plain old Rhiannon, scared of her own shadow. She wanted more than that, was just coming to realize that she *deserved* more than that—if she was brave enough to take it.

"I'm not sure about that blue. Give me a second." For several minutes, Camille rummaged around in the huge tackle box she used to hold her pedicure supplies, before finally coming out with two choices. One was a bright, electric purple and the other was a deep, rich turquoise.

"Either of these will look great with your complexion," she said, holding the bottles out to Rhiannon. "Which one do you like?"

Rhiannon started to take the purple—at least it was close to a color that normal people might wear, but something stopped her at the last second. Maybe it was the fact that she was tired of blending in, tired of being the wallflower after having spent three years perfecting the look.

"Give me the turquoise."

"All right! Rhiannon's taking a walk on the wild side. That's going to look fabulous."

"I hope so."

"I know so. And I'm an artist, so you should trust me."

"You drive a yellow car."

"Hey, don't insult Sunny. She's very sensitive."

"She's in the driveway."

"Yes, but she has great hearing."

Rhiannon cracked up—there was nothing like an afternoon with Camille to tickle her funny bone. Silence reigned for the next few minutes as both women concentrated on polishing their toes.

"So, you never really answered me." Camille finally broke the silence. "How is the graphic novelist?"

"He's doing well. Finishing up his latest novel."

"Oh, yeah? Have you seen him recently?"

"Yes."

"Really? Where? What did you guys do? Tell me everything."

"I don't know, we've done a lot of things."

Camille's eyes widened. "So you're dating him? Like seriously *dating* him?"

"I don't know how serious it is, but we see each other pretty regularly."

"How regularly?"

"What is this, the Spanish Inquisition?"

"Oh, come on. Give the old married woman a thrill."

"You have blue toes and purple hair—I'm not sure how much of a thrill my dating life is compared to that."

"Rhiannon! Come on. How often do you see him?"

Because she wouldn't mind Camille's take on the situation, Rhiannon relented. "Just about every day."

"Wait, let me get this straight. You see this man— Hey, what's his name?"

"Shawn."

"Right. So you see Shawn every day and you don't know if it's serious? I think that's the definition of serious, sweetie."

"I don't think that's necessarily true. You saw Matt every day for almost two months and then ran away to Rio. How serious was that?"

"Very serious. Why do you think I ran to Rio? I couldn't deal with the way he made me feel. And that little jaunt to Brazil ended up putting both of us through a lot of hell before we got it all straightened out, so learn from my mistakes."

"I never said I wanted things to be serious between Shawn and me."

"Yeah, but you never said you didn't, either." Camille leaped to her feet. "If we're going to talk about men, it definitely calls for chocolate. I'll be right back."

Camille was as good as her word, returning in under a minute with a box of designer chocolates, which she held out to Rhiannon. She started to pass on them like she always did, but in the end couldn't resist the pretty, milk chocolate heart nestled in the center of the box.

"At least that's one thing being with Shawn has done for me. I've suddenly started shoving anything and everything I can find into my mouth."

"I've noticed you've put on a few pounds—it looks great on you."

"Yeah, but suddenly my wardrobe has gotten a bit snug."

"I'm sorry, did you say shopping?"

Rhiannon looked at her, confused. "No, I said—"

"Are you sure, because I'm fairly certain that's what I heard when you said your clothes were too snug. I'm thinking Barton Creek, here we come."

"Don't be ridiculous. The baby—"

"Matt's a big boy, he can watch the baby for a few hours. Besides, shopping will give us a chance to talk about Shawn and your seriously not-serious relationship."

Rhiannon started to protest—it had been a long time since she'd gone shopping just for the sheer pleasure of it. Most days, looking at herself, at her body, in the mirror did nothing but upset her. But Camille looked so pleased with the prospect of an afternoon at the mall that she couldn't bring herself to say no. After all, how bad could it be? She'd try on a few things and then watch as Camille did the rest.

"Okay. But I'm supposed to meet Shawn at his place at seven, so I have to make it home in time to change clothes."

"Ooh, another date. What a perfect excuse for a new outfit."

Rhiannon didn't bother protesting, simply gathered her shoes and purse and headed outside to Sunny as Camille went to tell Matt what was up.

CHAPTER FIFTEEN

THREE HOURS LATER, she was regretting her complacency. Camille had dragged her through half the stores at the mall in search of the perfect date outfit and now they were standing in the middle of a world-famous lingerie store as her sister-in-law grabbed every sexy bra-and-panty set she could get her hands on.

"I don't need new underwear," Rhiannon protested as Camille ushered her toward a dressing room.

"A woman rarely needs new anything. That doesn't mean she shouldn't indulge herself every once in a while. Besides, you definitely need something more kick-ass than your regular white cotton if you're going to wow him with that red number we picked up."

Rhiannon had spent the past hour contemplating returning that very same red number, still unsure how Camille had managed to talk her into it. It didn't show much skin, but the whole thing was a heart-stopping scarlet that pretty much screamed "Look at me, look at me." She might have worked her way around to wearing turquoise polish on her toes, but she wasn't sure she was ready for anything as attention-getting as that outfit.

Still, Camille was having so much fun dressing her that Rhiannon couldn't bring herself to argue. If nothing else, she'd bring the stuff back later and Camille would never have to be the wiser. "Okay, fine. Pick out a set to go under the red thing and I'll buy it."

"Don't you want to try it on first?"

The thought of stripping down and looking at herself—and her scars—in the three-way mirror was pretty much Rhiannon's idea of hell, so she had no desire to try anything on. It had been hard enough to get through the endless clothing changes Camille had insisted on at the department stores.

"My bra size hasn't changed since puberty, so I think I'm pretty much safe on that front."

"Still, I want to see. You'll look so pretty!"

"Not quite."

"You know, the scars really aren't—"

"It's fine," she interrupted. "Really. *I'm* fine." Before Camille could say anything else, Rhiannon grabbed the red bra-and-panty set and headed for the front counter. By that time she was so desperate to get out of the store that she didn't argue when Camille added three more sets—black, purple and turquoise—to her pile.

They were in the car headed home, her sister-in-law's trunk loaded down with an astounding number of packages, most of them Rhiannon's—before Camille tried to return to the subject of the fancy underwear—and her scars.

"You know, Rhiannon, the scars aren't nearly as bad as you think they are."

"I see them every day, Camille. I know exactly how bad they are."

"Yeah, but—" Camille took a deep breath, kept her eyes on the road and Rhiannon could tell she was struggling with what she wanted to say—or at least how she wanted to say it. Finally, when the silence between them had gotten uncomfortable, she said, "I think you might be seeing them through the filter of how you got them. Do you know what I mean?"

"No, I don't. And I have no desire to talk about this."

"I know you don't. That's why I've left you alone about it for so long. But, Rhiannon, the way you see yourself isn't just unhealthy. It's completely untrue."

"Really? Are the scars just a figment of my imagination?" They were stopped at a red light, so she deliberately pushed the sleeves of her sweater up to give Camille a good view of the thick bands of scar tissue that surrounded her wrists.

Camille didn't flinch, didn't apologize, didn't pretend not to look. She simply stared at the scars for a minute, then said, "So what?"

Nothing could have crushed Rhiannon more, nor made her angrier. "Yeah, it's easy for you to say when it's not your body. I lived through this, Camille. I felt the pain every day for months after it happened."

"I know you did, that's what I'm trying to say. To you, those aren't just scars—they're symbols of everything that bastard did to you. Every time you see them, you don't see the thin, white lines that exist. You see your own pain and humiliation."

"Exactly! Do you think I want the whole world to see them, to know what he did to me? To know what I let him do to me?"

"Let him do? He tied you up and nearly killed you, Rhiannon. You didn't *let* him do anything to you."

"You know what I mean." She turned and looked out the side window, praying for the ride to be over.

"I *do* know what you mean, and that's the problem.

You've been blaming yourself for what happened to you,
blaming yourself for the failure of your marriage—"

"No—"

"Yes!" Camille sighed. "I love you, Rhiannon. I
really do—I think of you as the sister I never had.
Which is why it's so hard to sit by and watch you beat
yourself up over something that is such a small part of
who you are.

"Those scars don't define you. They don't make you
any less beautiful or less talented or less intelligent.
They just make you feel bad and I can't stand to watch
it anymore. We spent all day trying on clothes that
cover you from head to toe and I don't understand why.
You're a beautiful, vibrant woman with an incredible
body. Why should you hide it because some monster
hurt you?"

"So you think I should wear a string bikini, so everyone can see what he did?"

"If you want to wear a bikini, why shouldn't you
wear one?"

"I don't want to wear one—that's the point."

"I know that. But I also know you don't want to bury
yourself in jeans and sweaters for the rest of your life,
either. I saw the way you looked at those cute little
sundresses and that fabulous purple halter top. But you
wouldn't go near them, let alone actually try them on. I
think that's a shame, especially since they would look
terrific on you."

Rhiannon didn't say anything, *couldn't* say anything.
If she opened her mouth, she was terrified that she
would start screaming and never stop.

But Camille was on a roll—or maybe she figured
she'd get everything out now so they never had to talk

about this again. Because instead of changing the subject, the next time she opened her mouth, it was to ask, "What does Shawn say about your scars?"

Rhiannon shook her head, as she still didn't trust her voice.

Camille glanced at her quickly before turning her attention back to the road. "He hasn't said anything at all?"

"He hasn't seen them."

"He hasn't seen *any* of them?"

Rhiannon glanced at the highway signs, trying to figure out how long until they made it back to Matt and Camille's so she could escape. She didn't want to talk about this, didn't want Camille to see how insecure she was over her feelings about Shawn.

But she couldn't keep quiet, either. Now that someone was talking to her—really talking to her about the subject instead of tiptoeing around it—she was like a deer in the headlights. She couldn't bring herself to step away.

Clearing her throat, she murmured, "He saw the ones on my arms but that was on our first date and he's never mentioned them."

"I'm sorry, you've been dating this hot, younger guy for almost a month and you haven't slept with him?"

Rhiannon blushed. "It's not that simple."

"I've dated a lot of guys in my life. I'm sure I can keep up." She paused. "Are you worried about letting him see you? Or is it that you're worried about just being with him? I mean, I can't even imagine how difficult it would be—"

"He turned me down."

"What?" Camille nearly rear-ended the car in front of her. "He didn't want to…"

"I don't know. I mean, he seems to want to. And I think I want to, but the one time I invited him in, he told me he didn't think I was ready yet."

"*Were* you ready?"

"I thought I was. I don't know. I mean, I was scared but I also wanted to try. It was my fortieth birthday and he'd taken me out for this beautiful, romantic dinner. I was relaxed and happy and I thought, maybe it could work."

"And he said he didn't think you were ready, despite how you felt?" Camille looked outraged on her behalf.

She couldn't believe she was talking about this—and with her brother's wife, of all people. But she didn't know who else to ask for advice. Logan was her closest friend but somehow she couldn't see laying this problem in his lap. He'd probably have a coronary—and if he didn't, she would.

Deciding to lay everything out and get Camille's honest opinion on the situation, she said, "He could tell I was afraid, I guess, because he said that we would only try when my desire outweighed my fear."

"Wow. He really said that?"

"Yeah."

"You know he's a keeper, don't you? When you find a man who cares more about you than he does about himself…"

"I know. That's what I'm afraid of."

"Why afraid?"

"Well, I mean, when we started this whole thing, we were planning on keeping it casual. With the age difference and our priorities, it seemed smart. Only, now I'm feeling things that are distinctly uncasual."

"I can imagine." Camille reached over and patted her leg. "But I bet he is, too."

"You can't know that."

"Sure I can. If he didn't care about you—and the future the two of you could have together—he never would have walked away when you offered to put him out of his misery."

"I didn't exactly phrase the invitation like that."

"Maybe not, but the intention was obviously the same. And the fact that he didn't take you up on it, the fact that he wanted to wait until you were less vulnerable, proves that he's a good guy and that he's in this for more than kicks and giggles."

"Yeah, but what do I do? I mean, I'm still afraid of being with him. Of showing him the scars and facing all his questions. I think that I'll always be afraid, at least until we actually make love."

"Of course you will—I would think that that's only natural when a woman's been through everything that you have."

"So how do I convince him that I want to be with him? That I'm not doing it just for him?"

"Oh, sweetie, have you ever come to the right place. Listen up and I'll tell you *exactly* what to do."

RHIANNON WAS NERVOUS as she stopped her car at the top of Shawn's driveway. Was she really going to do this? she asked herself as she climbed out of the car and walked toward the front door, her steps faltering and unsure as she tried desperately to talk herself out of—or into—what she was about to do.

Every instinct she had for self-preservation told her to run, told her she was being crazy and stupid and completely presumptuous. But she couldn't stop, not now that she was here. If she did, she knew she'd never work up the nerve to do this again.

And she needed to do it—for herself and for Shawn. They couldn't go on the way they had been for the past couple of weeks, holding hands and kissing when both of them were so hot for each other they were on the verge of spontaneous combustion.

Ever since her fortieth birthday, being with Shawn had been a slow kind of torture—every nerve ending in her body was painfully alive, her hormones zipping around like a frog on speed. For a woman who had spent nearly three years in her own version of a sensory deprivation chamber, the pain—and the pleasure—of her newfound arousal was nearly overwhelming.

Despite what she'd said to Camille, Rhiannon knew Shawn felt the tension, too. Though he never pushed her, never asked her for more than she willingly gave, she knew how hard it was for him to leave at the end of each date.

She wanted more for him, more for herself. More for them, than this half relationship that was bringing her both incredible joy and incredible frustration. She was ready to concentrate on the joy for a while, and to leave the agony behind once and for all.

But could she do it? she wondered as she forced herself to take the last few steps leading up to Shawn's front door. Could she really put the fear aside and make love to him as she so desperately wanted to? She didn't know, but she was going to use their date tonight to find out, one way or the other.

Beneath her sweater, the new purple lace bra Camille had talked her into buying sizzled against her skin, and not for the first time, she wished she'd stuck to her plain old white cotton. She'd put on the fancy underwear, hoping it would give her confidence, but who was she kidding? With the way her body looked, it was absurd to think that showing it off in purple lace was a good idea. She'd be lucky if Shawn didn't run screaming into the night at his first glimpse of her, no matter what Camille said.

God knew, the scars had bothered Richard so much that the few times they'd tried unsuccessfully to make love, he'd insisted that they do it in the dark. He'd said it was because he couldn't concentrate when he looked at the scars, that they reminded him of everything she had suffered, but even then she'd known the truth. He'd been disgusted by the damage done to her body and hadn't been able to look at what his once-attractive wife had become.

Shawn wouldn't do that to her, Rhiannon reassured herself firmly as she rang his doorbell. He was nothing like Richard and she knew he would never hurt her the way her ex-husband had at the end of their marriage.

But did that mean he wouldn't feel like Richard had—repulsed by the mere sight of her—or only that he wouldn't show it? The thought sent a new wave of panic racing through her and it was all she could do to hold herself still and upright on the porch. If she hadn't already rung the stupid doorbell, she probably would have called with some ridiculous excuse.

As this thought occurred to her, the door swung open to reveal a deliciously rumpled Shawn. Dressed in ratty jeans and a faded Led Zeppelin T-shirt, with his feet bare and his too-long hair falling into his eyes, he looked relaxed and comfortable, not to mention sexy as all get out.

"Hey there." His smile was slow and sweet and so hot her stomach clenched at the sight of it.

"Hey yourself." She went into his arms with a grin of her own, pressed her face to the side of his neck and breathed in the dark sandalwood scent of him. He smelled so good that she stood there for a second, rubbing her nose back and forth against his skin as she took him deep inside her.

"What are you doing?" he asked, his tone amused.

"Sniffing you. You smell fantastic."

He laughed. "You smell pretty great yourself."

He started to step back, but she clung to him, her fingers wrapping around the hard muscles of his biceps as she pressed her body against his.

"Hey, are you okay?" he asked, tilting her head up so he could look in her eyes.

"I'm fabulous," she answered, and was shocked to realize that it was true. Much of her nervousness had dissipated upon seeing him and now all she felt was the happiness, the comfort, that came from being around him. "I just want to hold you for a minute. Is that okay?"

"It's better than okay." He squeezed her to him, rubbed his cheek against the top of her head.

She pulled back, looked him in the eyes. "Kiss me, Shawn."

"My pleasure, sweetheart."

With a grin, he lowered his mouth to hers, brushed his lips over hers, once, twice. But that wasn't the kind of kiss she wanted from him, not now when her body was on fire with the need to feel his bare skin against her own.

Sliding her hands up his neck, she tangled them in his hair and tugged him closer, until his mouth was pressed against hers. He tasted like sun-warmed forests and rich, exotic tea and she wanted more. Needed more. Opening her mouth, she deepened the kiss, sweeping her tongue over his lips before playing with the little indention in the middle of his bottom lip.

His mouth was soft and sweet and patient, so she took her time and explored every part of him, from his wicked, wild tongue to the recesses of his mouth. And when she finally let him go, every muscle in his body was rock-hard with desire and his eyes were nearly black, his pupils dilated wide. "Well, that was one hell of a hello kiss," he said, running a hand over his now swollen mouth.

She gave him the look she'd spent the better part of an hour perfecting in front of her vanity table mirror. "That was only the beginning."

CHAPTER SIXTEEN

SHAWN WASN'T SURE WHAT had gotten into Rhiannon, but he liked it. A lot. Her lush mouth was slicked with a soft pink lip gloss that looked amazing on her and her hair was tousled from where his fingers had run through it. She looked sexy and sweet and smelled absolutely wonderful

Pulling her deeper into the house, he closed the door behind her and then pressed her back against it. "So, to what do I owe such a warm greeting?"

"I missed you today."

"Did you?" He leaned down, nibbled his way down her neck to the sexy curve of her shoulder.

"You have no idea. My sister-in-law dragged me shopping and all I could think about was how much more fun I could be having over here, with you."

His heart warmed at her confession—and it wasn't the only part of his body feeling the heat. She'd only just arrived and already he was so hard he could barely think of anything but stripping her out of her clothes and making love to her.

"Shopping, hmm? Did you buy anything interesting?"

"I did, actually." She took his hand, slid it under her sweater until his palm cupped her breast. She must have been wearing some kind of demi-bra thing because only the bottom half of her breast was covered. He flexed his fingers, met warm, resilient flesh and nearly lost control right there.

He jerked, started to pull away, but her hand stroked over his, held him in place and Shawn swore nothing had ever felt so good.

He moved his palm a little, caressed the underside of her breast as his thumbs stroked over the plump upper curve. He wanted to see her, to taste her so badly that he was actually shaking with the need. But he knew how sensitive she was, how wary, and he contented himself with stroking his thumb over her nipple. Once, twice, then again and again as she shuddered and arched into his hand.

"Do you like it?" she asked, breathless.

"I love it," he growled, his fingers tightening on her before he could stop himself.

Her laugh was low, husky. "I meant the bra."

"Oh. Did you get a new bra?"

"I did. Wanna see it?"

"I want to see you more." He lowered his head and claimed her mouth in a kiss that showed her just a little of the pent-up passion he had inside of him, the need for her that had been eating him alive for weeks now.

"And I want to see you." She ran her free hand down his jaw, stroked her fingers over his lips for one long, charged second. Arched her back so that her nipple was a hard bud against his palm.

"Geez, Rhiannon. What are you doing to me?" he groaned as his knees actually trembled, something that had never happened to him before.

She licked her strawberry-tinted lips, smiled a wicked, wonderful smile that had heat shooting straight to his erection and whispered, "Trying to seduce you. Is it working?"

He pressed his lower hips against hers, let her feel how hard she made him. "Do you even have to ask?"

"Then take me."

"Are you sure? Because I don't want to rush—"

She stopped him with her hand against his lips. "I don't want to talk about it. I just want you to make love to me."

The first alarm bells went off in the back of his head, but since most of the blood in his brain had moved about three and a half feet south, he didn't pay much attention to them. Couldn't pay attention to them, not when everything he had—everything he was—was focused on Rhiannon.

She ducked out from under his arm and started walking slowly backward across his entryway. Her eyes never left his as she crooked her finger in a blatant invitation, one he had absolutely no intention of turning down.

"Where's your bedroom?" She toyed with the small, pearl buttons on the front of her sweater.

"Down that hall." He couldn't take his eyes from her, not when she was suddenly the incarnation of every fantasy he'd ever had. He didn't know what had changed her mind, what had made her decide that she wanted him enough to take him, and at that moment he didn't care. All that mattered was being with her in any and every way that he could.

She turned toward his bedroom and he followed her, admiring the subtle sway of her nicely rounded rear end as she moved down the hall. He couldn't wait to peel her jeans off her, couldn't wait to fill his hands with her as he thrust deep inside her.

Images danced through his brain, and as they entered his darkened bedroom he reached for the light switch, needing to see her with a hunger that bordered on obsession.

"Don't," she murmured, stopping him by placing her long, cool fingers over his.

"I want to see you," he said, grabbing the belt loop of her jeans and pulling her flush against him. "I've dreamed about what you looked like for so long."

"Next time."

The alarm bells were getting louder, despite his arousal, and this time he tried to talk to her. "Rhiannon, are you sure you're ready for this? We can wait—"

Her hands came up between them, her palms against his chest, and she pushed him, hard. Caught off balance, he tumbled sideways onto the bed and then she was crawling over him, straddling him. Any thoughts he had about anything went right out of his head as she peeled his T-shirt over his head.

"Does this feel like I want to wait?" she asked, running her hands all over his naked torso.

"No," He barely choked the word out.

"Exactly." She leaned down, took his nipple in her mouth and he almost shot straight off the bed.

"Easy, baby," he murmured, as she circled him with her tongue, sending shards of pleasure shooting through him at an alarming rate. "Slow down or this will be over before it starts."

"What if I don't want to slow down?" She trailed her lips over his chest, then licked her way down the rigid plane of his abdomen. She paused at his navel, circling it with her tongue again and again before moving lower and pressing kisses along the line of his jeans. "I've waited just as long for you as you have for me, you know."

Her words shot through him, eliminating his resistance and making him throb with the need to be inside her.

"Do whatever you want," he groaned. "But do it fast or I'm going to—"

The pop of his jeans button opening echoed through the room, had him holding his breath as he waited to see what Rhiannon was going to do next. Hell, he couldn't believe what she'd already done. Where was the shy woman from whom he'd had to coax a response? The woman who had run away the first time he'd kissed her?

He liked this new Rhiannon, this temptress who seduced instead of being seduced, but at the same time, he didn't understand where she'd come from, didn't understand why she was doing what she was doing.

But then she lowered his zipper and any thoughts he'd managed to hang on to flew right out of his head, until the only thing he was aware of was the blinding need for completion.

She pulled his jeans down his legs, lingering in numerous places to kiss and lick and touch until he was sure he would go out of his mind.

His hands found hers in the darkness and he murmured, "Stop, please. I want to touch you, too."

"Next time," she whispered, again.

He jackknifed into a sitting position, did his best to ignore the throbbing arousal that was making each breath agony. "What do you mean, next time? I want to make love to you, Rhiannon, not be some boy toy for you to play with!"

Her laugh was low and husky and so close to his erection that her exhalations caressed him like a thousand tiny fingers. "My boy toy?" she whispered. "Is that what you are?"

Her lips closed over him before he could answer, and then he couldn't answer, couldn't think. Couldn't do anything but savor her as she made love to him with her mouth.

He looked down the length of his body, tried to make out her face in the dim light, strained to see the crazy mixed-up colors of her hair, but it was too dark and all he could do was feel.

Feel as she slid her lips up and down his length. Feel as her tongue swirled around him again and again. Feel as her cool fingers cupped him between his legs.

"Rhiannon, please."

"Please what?" she whispered before taking all of him into her mouth again.

"Stop. I'm close, baby. Too close. I want to be inside you when it happens, want to feel you and kiss you the way you've done to me."

She murmured a sound that could have been an assent, but then she didn't stop. Instead, she just kept turning him inside out, one slow lick at a time.

SHAWN'S WORDS SHOT through Rhiannon, turning her on even more than she already was. She could do this, she told herself, more relieved than she could have believed possible. She *was* doing this—making love to Shawn like she'd fantasized about and he was enjoying it.

Anxiety was still a fist in her stomach, but even that had gotten better, evened out some as she concentrated on touching Shawn and his beautiful, beautiful body. She wanted to see him, wished she could risk turning the light on so she could see all the flat planes and hollows she was learning by touch. But she knew, eventually, she'd have to take her clothes off and she still couldn't stand the idea of Shawn seeing her scars.

Maybe she had no business making love to him if she wasn't able to open herself completely to him, but no one had said she had to give him everything all at once. She couldn't. Right now, the fact that she was here, touching him and not freaking out, would have to be enough— for both of them.

Closing her eyes, she concentrated on bringing him as much pleasure as she could. She wanted him to enjoy this, *needed* him to enjoy it. Needed to know that she was capable of bringing him pleasure, no matter how messed up she was inside.

"Rhiannon." His voice was a husky plea and she reveled in it, pouring everything she had into bringing him more and more pleasure. She moaned low in her throat, smiling inwardly as he almost came off the bed, then reached up and scraped her nails down his abdomen—not hard enough to leave a mark, just enough to ratchet the pleasure up another notch.

"Baby, come on, stop. I'm too close."

She wanted him close, wanted to take him all the way with her mouth and her hands because she wasn't sure she was ready to take him into her body yet. There was still too much pain associated with the act in her mind, still too many bad memories for her to relish the act of lovemaking itself. But being in control as she brought Shawn pleasure, what was there not to like about that?

"Rhiannon." It was a command and a plea, an order and a suggestion and she ignored them all—until Shawn's fingers tightened in her hair.

Panic skated through her, ice-cold and razor-sharp. "What are you doing?" she whispered frantically, trying to get back to the warm, pleasurable place she'd been only moments before.

His hands went to her ribcage and he lifted her off him, rolling in one smooth motion until she was beneath him and he was between her legs, his erection pressing against the soft denim of her blue jeans.

"My turn," he said, his mouth skimming down her neck to her shoulder.

Little shoots of pleasure worked their way through her, warred with the fear slowly invading her veins. It was going to be okay, she told herself. This was Shawn. He wouldn't hurt her, wouldn't do anything she didn't want.

She repeated the words to herself as he slowly divested her of her bra and sweater, turned them into a mantra as he slid her jeans and panties down her legs. She could do this, she could do this, she could do this.

"Hey, are you okay?" Shawn asked, and she knew he was straining to see her through the darkness.

"I'm great." She ran a hand over his shoulders to reassure him, squeezed the strong muscles of his back as he leaned in to kiss her.

His mouth was hard on hers, demanding, and she tried to lose herself to the desire she could feel emanating from him in waves. Sliding her hands up his back to

his head, it was her turn to tangle her hands in his hair
and tug until he reluctantly relinquished her mouth.

She gasped for breath, tried to focus, tried to stay
in the present despite the memories ripping through
her. Memories of another man with a hard mouth and
well-developed muscles.

Shawn braced his arms on either side of her, caging
her in, trapping her. Dread welled up inside of her, took
her over, but she tried to fight it. This was Shawn, she
told herself over the thundering in her ears. This was
Shawn, she tried to remember as her blood raced with
remembered horror. This was Shawn, this was Shawn,
this was Shawn. Again and again, she reminded herself
who was above her, kissing her, touching her, loving
her.

But when he settled between her legs, his erection nudging at the very heart of her, alarm slammed
through her in a frenzied rush. She started to scream,
her fists and feet and body flailing against him as hysteria set in.

CHAPTER SEVENTEEN

SHAWN WAS PRETTY DAMN close to hysteria himself as he rolled off Rhiannon and fumbled for the lights. He finally managed to switch on the bedside lamp and as his eyes adjusted to the sudden brightness, his first good look at her wrecked him.

She was sobbing silently, every part of her shaking with the intensity of her pain and fear. Her mascara made watery black streaks down her cheeks and her entire body was flushed a deep rose that only accentuated the thin white lines that zagged and curled over her arms and shoulders.

She was clutching his sheet to her chest with one hand but she was so upset that it slipped with every harsh sob that wracked her slender body, giving him a view of her breasts and upper abdomen that sent fury rampaging through him even as he wondered if he'd been expecting it. How naive would it have been for him to have seen the damage to her arms and not realized that it covered other, more vulnerable parts of her body?

The knowledge that he *had* subconsciously known about her other injuries did nothing to soothe his rage—or the horror winding its way through him as he watched Rhiannon struggle to get control of herself.

How could he have not known she was working

herself into this state? How could he have been making love to her, letting her make love to him, and not realized just how panic-stricken she had become?

He felt like a heel, like a monster, like a complete and total asshole as he sat there, watching her battle demons he couldn't even imagine, demons he couldn't begin to fight.

He wanted to help Rhiannon but he didn't know how, didn't know if reaching out to her would calm her down or just make her suffering worse. But not touching her was killing him, so he reached out one hand, making sure to move slowly and give her plenty of time to stop him.

When she didn't, some of the ice that had formed around his heart began to melt and he softly began to stroke her hair.

"Baby, can you hear me?" He kept his voice calm when what he really wanted to do was rage and curse. "Rhiannon? It's me, Shawn. Are you with me? You're safe, sweetheart. I promise, you're safe. I won't hurt you. I won't let anything happen to you."

She didn't answer, but then he hadn't expected her to. When Cynthia had lapsed into hysterics, she hadn't been able to form a coherent sentence for hours. Still, when Rhiannon didn't pull away, he sank down onto the bed next to her.

"Come on, sweetheart. You've got to calm down. You're going to make yourself sick."

She didn't respond and her sobs didn't abate, but she allowed him to pull her against his chest. Her arms went around his neck and she buried her face in the curve of his shoulder and sobbed like her heart was breaking wide-open.

"I'm sorry. I'm so sorry, Rhiannon. I never meant to hurt you."

His words only made her cry harder.

Because he didn't know what else to do, he rocked her back and forth, making soothing, unintelligible noises. Murmuring to her, trying to convince her—and himself—that everything was going to be all right.

He'd been down this path before, maybe never quite like this, but he'd seen Cynthia in depressions this bad—maybe even worse. Had learned a million tricks to snap her out of them and he tried them all here, to no avail. Eventually, he just gave up and let Rhiannon cry.

Time passed slowly as his mind whirled through everything that could have happened to her, everything that could have brought her to this state. Each possibility was more unpleasant than the next and he kicked himself again and again for not seeing that he was bringing things back. For not calling a halt to their lovemaking before she'd gotten to this state.

He'd known that something was wrong, damn it, had sensed it almost from the first. But he hadn't stopped her, hadn't even tried to stop her after the first few minutes. He'd been too caught up in what she was doing to him, in how she was making him feel. In the thrill of the realization that he would finally be able to hold her and love her like he wanted to.

Love her? What a sad, pathetic joke that thought was. He'd nearly broken her.

Shawn didn't know how long they sat there, rocking, but when Rhiannon had finally calmed enough to pull away, her eyes were nearly swollen shut.

"I'm sorry," she said, her voice lower and more

expressionless than he had ever heard it. "God, Shawn, I'm so sorry."

"Please, Rhiannon, don't say that to me. Say anything else, call me a bastard, hit me, do whatever you need to do, but please don't tell me that *you're* sorry. I'm the one who—"

"Don't take this on yourself. It's all my fault—you had nothing to do with it."

He wanted to argue—*would* argue later as he hated how easily she took all the blame on herself—but he was smart enough to figure out that now wasn't the time. Right now, she needed acceptance, not opposition.

"Do you want to tell me what happened?" he asked softly.

"Not really. But I guess I owe you an explanation, don't I?"

"You don't owe me anything you don't want to give me—I thought I'd made that clear before now." He paused, struggling for the right words. Finally, he settled on the truth. "You don't need to push yourself. I'm okay with waiting—"

"Aww, Shawn, I keep telling you my little freak-out wasn't about you, but you're just not hearing me."

"It's pretty hard to believe that when I was the one on top of you when you lost it. If I did anything to hurt you, I'm so very sorry."

"You didn't do anything. You were perfect, amazing. I loved touching you."

But not being touched by him. He noticed the distinction, filed it away to think about later. Right now he needed every ounce of concentration his rattled nerves could muster to negotiate his way through the sudden minefield of their relationship.

"I'll tell you about it—about him, if you want to know."

Everything inside of him froze, then tightened to the point of pain. It was like the entire world, or at least his corner of it, had shrunk to fit into that one sentence. He wanted to hear the story so badly he could taste it, needed to know who had hurt her so powerfully that it was like poisoned claws raking away at his insides.

"I want to know."

She nodded, then hitched the sheet up higher around herself, as if it would protect her from what she was about to do. As if she needed whatever armor she could find.

"Do you want to get dressed first?" he asked.

"I just want to get it over with. If I wait too long, I'll completely lose my nerve."

The need for revenge ripped through him and his anger swelled until it was all he could do to sit still. He wanted to hit something, wanted to hurt someone as badly as Rhiannon was hurting. As badly as he was hurting. It was an odd feeling for a man who had always considered himself a pacifist, and that much more powerful because of its complete and utter strangeness.

Cursing under his breath, he bent down and retrieved his beloved Led Zeppelin shirt from where it had landed beside the bed, then pulled it down over her head before she even realized his intentions. It wasn't much, but surely it was better than her sitting there, naked and vulnerable, before him.

Yet as he looked at her, he could have sworn he saw a new flicker of hurt in her eyes, one he could distinguish from the others by the depths of its intensity. He wanted to ask her about it, to demand to know what he had done to cause it, but just then she began to speak in a voice so low, so haunted, that it sent shivers down his spine.

"I used to be a journalist. In fact, I spent all of my adolescence and most of my adult life working for a newspaper."

"Did you like it?"

"I loved it, loved everything about it, from the scent of a lead to the smell of the ink as it hit the newsprint." She sighed. "And I was good at it—really, really good at it.

"Within two years of graduating from college I'd worked my way up from a small biweekly to the *Austin American-Statesman*. Within another three, I'd moved from covering the social beat to being in charge of the crime beat.

"Most days it was so much damn fun I could hardly believe it—like a game that no one knew how to win, but that everyone wanted to master. By the end of my time there, I was the paper's number one investigative reporter. I was chasing down leads all day, every day—real leads, bogus ones. It didn't matter, I got them. And I ran them all down, even the ones that were obviously false. Better to check a story out than to miss something big."

From his research, he knew some of this already—a lot of it, actually—but it was different hearing it from her. It made everything more real, including what he was deathly afraid was coming next.

"Anyway, when I was thirty-four, the AP came calling and I couldn't say no. They wanted me to move to a bigger bureau, to Dallas or Philadelphia or Phoenix, but my husband's job was here. Our life was here. So

I cut a deal—I'd spend most of my time working out of the Austin office, but if anything big happened in Dallas or Houston, I would be there, the same day.

"It worked for a while, but then I was spending more and more time in Dallas, because that's where the stories were. In a lot of ways, Austin is still a small town, with a small town's problems—which is great, if you live here. Not so great if the AP wants you to make a name for yourself covering murder and mayhem."

The bad part was coming, he could feel it from the way she had begun to tremble once again, and from the look in her eyes. When she'd been talking about reporting, they'd been a clear, bright copper but now they were muddy and shadowed as she took one shuddering breath after another.

"Anyway, the AP wanted me to cover the big news stories, but I'm—or at least I was—an investigative reporter at heart. So when I got wind of a major cover-up that a U.S. senator from Dallas was involved in, I couldn't let it go. Richard told me not to get involved, he told me I was playing with both of our lives, but I was on the scent. The people have a right to know what their elected officials are up to." She snorted. "I was still naive enough to believe that credo back then."

He waited long seconds for her to continue, but she didn't. She had gone somewhere in her head that he couldn't follow and it took a while before she remembered that she was in the middle of a story that had him on tenterhooks—in the most horrible way imaginable.

"I was staying in Dallas to research the story— at this crappy motel my bureau chief always put me up in. Richard always hated that, said that we could afford better and to hell with what the AP wanted. After the—" Her voice faltered, broke and she cleared her throat before trying again. "After the rape, he used to tell me that he'd told me so. That it never would have happened if I'd been staying at a decent place."

She shook her head, picked at imaginary lint on his sheet. "I don't know. Maybe he was right."

Shawn was still reeling from having his suspicions confirmed, his brain replaying her words over and over again. Rhiannon had been raped. Brutally, horribly raped if the scars on her body were any indication. Anger churned inside him as he thought of her bastard of an ex-husband leaning over her battered body and saying some version of "I told you so."

"What happened?" He grated the words out between clenched teeth. He didn't sound anywhere near as sympathetic as he wanted to, but at that moment there was no sympathy in his body. No empathy. All he wanted to know was who had hurt Rhiannon—and where to find them.

"It's not exactly an original story, which somehow makes it worse, you know? I was stupid, arrogant, thought I could handle anything that came my way with my forty hours of self-defense training. What a joke. I never even saw it coming.

"I'd worked late at the office, trying to track down a source who had given me information and then completely disappeared from sight. I found out later that they had killed him—he wasn't the kind of guy anyone would notice going missing—but at that point, I just wanted to find him. I needed him to help put together the pieces of my huge story." Her voice turned mocking. "It seems so ridiculous saying that now, knowing how things turned out."

He wanted to ask what she meant, but he had a sick feeling he knew. One of the U.S. senators was from Dallas, and had been in the Senate for over fifteen years—which meant Rhiannon's story had never gone to print. Everything she'd done, everything she had sacrificed, everything that had been taken from her, had been for nothing.

The unfairness of it made his skin burn and his blood boil.

"Anyway, on my way back to the motel, I noticed that someone was following me in a black SUV—or at least, I thought they were following me. It was hard to tell because the road was dark and still relatively crowded, despite the fact that it was close to midnight.

"I stopped at a busy convenience store, filled up with gas. Tried to find him, you know, to get a plate number, but he was gone.

"He got me, twenty minutes later, walking from my car to my room. I thought I'd lost him—actually, I had convinced myself that the idea of anyone following me was nothing but childish fear."

She laughed, but the sound held no humor. "Boy, when I get it wrong. He was one of my sources on a story—one of the big sources who had been feeding me bits and pieces for weeks. Stringing me along, I realize now, but at the time, he'd been so sincere, so earnest. I'd believed him when he said he couldn't live with what the senator was doing, his conscience wouldn't let him sleep. It turned out he'd been sniffing around, trying to figure out how much I knew—how much I'd passed on—before he shut me up.

"He hit me on the head and dragged me into my room when I was still too confused from the head injury to fight. Then he tied me to the bed, which— lucky me—had a very accommodating headboard with slats in it. He had to get creative with the legs as there was no footboard, but he managed."

Her eyes were far away again and he knew she had gone back to that time, to that moment, and he couldn't stand it. Couldn't stand knowing that she was sitting next to him, that he was holding her, but she was completely out of his reach. In those moments she belonged to a sadistic monster more than she had ever belonged to him and he wanted nothing in the world so much as to bring her back to the present. To get her as far away from the torturous pain of her past as he could manage.

"Rhiannon, that's enough." He barely recognized his voice. It had gone deeper, turned feral, and the only thing he wanted more than to bring Rhiannon back to him was to spend ten minutes alone with the man who had totally and utterly destroyed the woman she had been.

She didn't respond, so lost in the past that he doubted if she'd even heard him. "I'm sure you can guess the rest, right? He gagged me, cut me—" she held out her arms so he could see the cuts, as if he didn't already have each and every one of them memorized "—told me that I was digging into things that I had no business being involved in.

"He said he'd been sent to teach me a lesson—and boy, did he ever. When he was done—when he was done, he stabbed me in the abdomen and the side. Not deep enough to kill me but deep enough to make me bleed like a stuck pig. One more punishment for sticking my nose where it didn't belong. And then he left me and I lay there, for ten hours, bleeding and covered in his filth, praying. To this day, I don't know if I was praying to live—or to die.

"For a while, I tried to attract attention. I rocked the bed, banged it against the wall, but it was my bad luck that the rooms on either side of me were empty. So no one found me until the maid came in to clean at eleven o'clock. She didn't take it well."

He didn't need to ask how Rhiannon had taken it. She was no longer a journalist, no longer married, no longer able to see herself as the beautiful woman she was. How much of her blindness was due to the scars, he wondered, and how much because of the brutality of the attack?

And he had rolled her over, pinned her beneath him, held her wrists in his hand as he all but ripped the clothes from her body. Was it any wonder she had freaked out? If he could reach it, he would kick his own ass.

But he couldn't, so he had to settle for a totally lame, completely ineffectual apology. "I'm so sorry, Rhiannon."

She looked surprised. "Why are you sorry? You didn't do anything to hurt me."

No, but he hadn't done anything to heal her, either, even knowing how hurt she was. Before tonight he might not have known the extent of the atrocities she'd endured, but he'd guessed that she'd been attacked and still he had brought her up to his room.

"The only reason I even told you was because I freaked out like that. I wanted you to understand that

it wasn't anything you'd done. That it was me. All me."
She closed her eyes and he hated the fact that he'd
lost that window into her thoughts. Into her state of
mind.

"You know, I wasn't always like this. I used to
be brave and put-together, really adventurous, you
know. Even after the rape, I tried to hold it together—
for Richard, for work, for myself. But when he was
acquitted—"

"The bastard who hurt you isn't in jail." It was a
statement, not a question.

She shook her head. "No. Like I told you, I'd worked
the crime beat for years, so I knew a lot of cops, had
a pretty good relationship with them. After the details
of what had happened to me circulated, they went out
of their way to find a way to charge him. He had an
airtight alibi for the night, plus plenty of reasons to
explain the trace evidence that placed him in my hotel
room. After all, he'd been there before, discussing the
case with me. He was sorry about what had happened
to me, but the trauma had obviously pushed me around
the bend. He was well-respected, a senator's aide. He
would never—" Her voice broke, but she continued.

"He would never do anything like that. It became a
case of his word against mine, and though the police
believed me, they couldn't nail him. They grew frustrated, were overzealous and he got off on a chain-of-
evidence technicality. Not to mention the fact that there
were allegations of police brutality.

"The funny part was, if I hadn't been the victim, I
would have been all over that story—police damaging
suspect in quest for rapist. It has a good ring to it."

Shawn didn't think it was funny—he thought it was

awful. Beneath the calm mask he wore, his stomach rolled and pitched. He didn't think he could take any more, but in the end, he didn't have a choice. It turned out Rhiannon wasn't quite done.

Looking straight at him, her brown eyes eerily calm, she said, "When that happened, it broke something inside me. Broke me. It's been almost three years and I still haven't been able to put myself back together again. I don't think I ever will."

CHAPTER EIGHTEEN

"YOU AREN'T BROKEN." Shawn's voice was firm, his eyes resolute as he stared down at her.

"Really?" Rhiannon forced herself to adopt a who-gives-a-damn tone. "I went home a couple of weeks ago and trashed my apartment. I quit journalism and became a party planner because I couldn't do the job anymore. I talked you into making love to me and then wigged out the second you actually tried to do what I asked for. What would you call me? A tease, maybe, except I don't think I've left you very titillated."

"Stop making jokes about it," he ground out.

"Well, it's either that or cry again and you're all out of tissues."

"Rhiannon, stop! You don't need to do this with me." He'd never yelled at her before, and his tone gave her pause, but only for a moment. She was done being vulnerable, done making a total and complete idiot of herself in front of this man.

"I'm not doing it for you. I'm doing it for me."

"Really?" The look he gave he was patently disbelieving. "How's that working out for you?"

"Better than the alternative." She started to stand, to walk away, but then realized she was only wearing his old shirt. If she went anywhere he would see—in stark detail—just what had been done to her. And after everything that had happened in the past hour, she didn't think she could take that humiliation on top of everything else.

He hadn't been able to stand looking at the scars on her chest and shoulders, had covered her up to hide them. How would he feel if he could see her back and bottom?

But staying here, on this bed—with him, was also out of the question. Because, despite everything, she still wanted him. Still needed him to hold her and comfort her and make her feel safe. She hadn't felt safe in three long years, but those moments, when he'd held her while she cried, had come the closest.

"Do you know where my clothes are?" she asked, quietly. "I need to get dressed so I can leave. I'm so sorry I wasted your time."

"Where do you think you're going?"

She bristled at his tone, though she figured she deserved it after everything she'd put him through tonight. "Home. I never planned on staying the night—you probably have things to do."

"The only thing I have to do tonight is to take care of you."

"That's the whole point. I don't want you to take care of me."

He shrugged. "Then you shouldn't have come over tonight, bent on seducing me. Once a woman makes love to me, I pretty much feel I've got the right to take care of her if I want."

"We never made love."

"Close enough."

Why was he doing this? She was doing her best to keep it together, to let him off the hook without any hard feelings, but he wasn't taking the outs she was giving him. After everything was said and done, Richard had practically sprained an ankle in his headlong dash away from her. And now, here was Shawn with the whole sordid story in his lap and he hadn't so much as moved an inch. Nor had he let her move.

It was infuriating, disturbing. Nerve-racking in the extreme. Was she supposed to trust him now that he had seen the real her? Was she supposed to expect him to stick around and just accept this new version of her?

How could she, when no one else had?

On the best days, that kind of trust didn't come easy to her, and today definitely hadn't been a good day. It had been hard enough to come here and ask Shawn to make love to her, to trust that she would somehow make it through that step. And look how well that had turned out.

No, she had to get out of here. If not out of Shawn's house, then at least away from his knowing eyes for a little while. How else was she supposed to get her composure back? How else was she supposed to figure out how to move on after what had almost happened between them?

"Can I take a shower?" she asked abruptly. "I feel—" Dirty. Trapped. Exposed. Frightened. She didn't say them, but then she didn't have to. He could pick any negative adjective he wanted to fill in the blanks and probably get a good idea of what she was feeling. It was a good thing, too, as she couldn't bring herself to voice her emotions.

"Of course." Shawn jumped to his feet and she realized for the first time that he was still naked.

She averted her eyes, though a big part of her wanted to look her fill. He had a beautiful body, one she'd enjoyed touching very much. But it would have been nice to see him in decent light.

He disappeared for a second, came back wearing a thick navy blue robe that covered him from shoulder to shin. Even as messed up as she was, she couldn't help missing the view—just a little.

Her thoughts surprised her with their sexual bent, particularly considering the fact that she had just completely fallen apart—all because she'd felt his naked body on top of hers and for a minute hadn't been able to distinguish the present from the past.

So how could she still be thinking of him that way?

"The bathroom's through here." He led her into a room that was about half the size of her very spacious condominium and she tried not to gape, especially when he turned on the shower and water came spurting out of six different heads.

"Hedonistic much?" she asked, watching as he adjusted the water temperature and the aim of the showerheads.

"If you've got it, flaunt it."

"Absolutely. Who cares about the environment, after all?" Where were these quips coming from and why couldn't she shut up, especially since he'd been nothing but kind to her?

"I have a water reclamation system—all the water from the shower is used to water the plants. So don't feel too bad about it, okay?"

"Sure." She reached over and casually turned the

main light off, leaving only the dim glow of the secondary light. He didn't say anything, but he stiffened. She was very glad she couldn't see the look in his eyes. She wasn't ready to handle any more questions, or criticisms.

"Thanks." She turned her back to him and waited for him to leave.

He obviously figured out that he'd been dismissed, because she heard the bathroom door open. "Call me if you need me," he said.

"I won't."

"Right." He cleared his throat. "There are towels in the cabinet to the left of the shower. Use as many as you'd like." The door closed behind him.

She stared at the running water for a while, trying to work up the energy to move, to think. But she was spent, numb, her emotions completely outside her control. Finally, when the room had almost completely steamed up from the hot water, she whipped his shirt off and held it to her nose.

It smelled like him—spicy and sexy and just a little sweet. For the first time since she'd gotten control of herself, emotions threatened to break through. She pushed them back, dropped the shirt. Feeling was dangerous.

But when she finally made it into the shower, it was as if she had forgotten what to do. She stood there, letting the water pour over her for long minutes. She didn't cry—there were no more tears left inside of her. There was nothing left inside her—she felt like a dried-out husk, like a statue whose heart and mind and soul had turned to stone.

Finally, because she could think of nothing else to

do, she sat down on the long bench that ran the length of the shower, pulled her knees up under her chin, and waited for the water to wash the dirt away.

WHAT WAS TAKING her so long? Shawn wondered as he paced the length of his bedroom. Back and forth, back and forth. He walked it again and again as he waited for the sound of the shower turning off, the sound of the bathroom door opening.

Finally, after close to half an hour, he knocked on the door. "Rhiannon, are you okay? Rhiannon? Rhiannon, answer me!" Visions of Cynthia hanging from that beam assailed him, followed by a crystal clear picture of his medicine cabinet—equipped with sleeping pills for the bout of insomnia he'd suffered the year before and his favorite five-blade razor.

"Damn it, Rhiannon, are you all right?" he shouted again. There was still no response, so he shoved the door open, terror a knife blade in his gut. When he saw her sitting under the shower, her arms wrapped around her bent knees, he felt a rush of relief followed by a quick surge of anger. Couldn't she have answered him?

But as he got closer to the shower, he realized that no, she couldn't have. She was completely zoned out—whether from shock or self-preservation, he didn't know.

Kicking off the shoes he'd put on when he'd re-dressed in an effort to make Rhiannon feel a little safer than she would with him in a robe, he opened the shower door and stepped in, fully dressed.

She didn't so much as blink. "Come on, baby," he

said, pulling her into his arms. "Let's get you out of here."

"Not yet," she said in a haunted voice. "I'm still dirty."

"Oh, Jesus." He closed his eyes for a moment, then let her slide to the ground next to him, making sure to keep an arm around her waist at all times, to stop her from falling. "Let's wash you, then."

He reached for a washcloth, once again movingly slowly so as not to spook her. "Do you want me to help you?"

For a long time she didn't answer, then finally she nodded once.

"All right." He reached for the shower gel, squeezed some onto the washcloth and then wrung it out.

"Come here, baby," he said, as he ran the washcloth over her shoulders and down her right arm, then her left, doing his best not to notice the scars she was so ashamed of. But the light in here was better than in the bedroom—even set on dim—and he could see the stark, white lines perfectly.

His stomach nearly revolted, not at how she looked but at the horror of what had been done to her.

He tried to keep his touch clinical as he washed her, tried not to notice her small, high breasts and the raspberry nipples that crowned them. It wasn't as difficult as he thought it would be, because with every inch of her body that he covered, he saw more scars, more evidence of injuries. More signs that she'd been brutalized.

It was torture for him, as he crouched at her feet, soaping her thighs and calves and feet. Images burned into his brain forever, pictures of her being tortured by a madman with a knife. When he turned her around to start on her back he saw the scars there that could only have been made by something striking her repeatedly and nearly lost it. Nearly dropped to his knees and sobbed himself.

But she didn't need pity from him—not now and maybe not ever. She was too strong for that, too proud. So he locked his own emotions away and concentrated on her.

Eventually, he'd soaped up her entire body with quick but gentle strokes of the washcloth and he reached for the nearest showerhead, pulled the wand out of the wall, and started rinsing her off.

When it was done, when she was completely rinsed off—completely cleaned—he reached to turn the shower off. "Come on, Rhiannon. Let's get you into bed."

"Not yet." Her hands clutched at his sodden shirt and he pulled her against him, ignoring the discomfort of his clothes and the icy heat of the fury that still burned within him. "I don't want to sleep yet. I'll have nightmares."

Of course she would. He'd scared the hell out of her tonight. Add in the fact that she'd relived the whole rape for him, was it any wonder she didn't want to sleep?

"Okay, no bed. That's fine. What do you want to do?"

"I want you to touch me."

He froze, certain he hadn't heard her correctly. After everything that had happened tonight, surely she hadn't just asked him to—

"Please, Shawn. I haven't been with a man in three years. Not since the rape."

God, how did she stand it? The pain was nearly overwhelming—it threatened to rip him in two. "Rhiannon, I don't think you mean that. You're upset and confused and—"

"I'm not an idiot! I know what I'm asking. I know I freaked out earlier, but I won't this time. I swear."

"You don't know that. I don't want to cause you any more pain."

"Don't you want me anymore? Is it the scars? You can turn the lights out—"

"Jesus, stop. Just stop!" The face she turned up to him was pale and tear-ravaged. It showed every one of her forty years and it was still the most beautiful thing he'd ever seen. He cupped her jaw in his palms. "I think I'll go to my grave wanting you, Rhiannon. You're strong and you're beautiful and I don't give a damn about your scars, except to hate that you suffered. But they're a part of you and they show how incredibly strong you really are. How could I be disgusted by them?"

"Richard was." Her voice was tiny.

"Richard sounds like he was almost as big a bastard as the man who did this to you and I do *not* appreciate being compared to him."

"I wasn't comparing you, I swear." She paused, then asked in a tiny voice, "But, if it isn't the scars, why won't you touch me again?"

"Because you nearly had a nervous breakdown in my arms two hours ago? Because I think you need to rest? Because I don't think you know what it is you're asking?"

"Please, Shawn. He's inside me and I can't get him out. He's been in me for three years, in my head and my body. In my soul. I just want to get him out. I just want him to leave me alone."

In his mind he went through every vile curse he could think of, and then some he was pretty sure he was making up as he went along. How could she ask this of him, now? He was still shaken by what had happened in the bedroom, and terrified that he would somehow bring her back to that state again. Terrified that he would somehow hurt her again.

He wanted to say no, to tell her they could try again when they had both had time to calm down. Now that he knew what had happened to her, things would be different. He would make them different.

But she was staring at him, her eyes huge and as dark as the night sky, and somehow he knew that turning her down now would shatter her completely.

Closing his eyes, he prayed that he was doing the right thing. Prayed that he had enough control to see this thing through without damaging Rhiannon any more than she had already been damaged.

Shrugging out of his shirt, he let it fall to the shower floor, then gathered her slender, shaking body against him. "Come here, sweetheart. Just let me hold you for a minute."

She clung to him, her arms wrapping around his waist as she buried her face against his chest. Without giving himself time to think about all the reasons this was a bad idea, he tilted her face up to his, then kissed her gently. The water was warm on his tongue as he licked his way over her mouth and down her neck to the hollow of her throat before kissing his way back up to the spot behind her ear that always made her melt.

She trembled against him and he reached behind

her, adjusting the showerheads so that they hit her more fully.

"I'm not cold."

"Shh. We're doing this my way." He kissed her to soften his words, sliding his hands up and down her back in a gentle caress meant to soothe them both.

He couldn't believe he was doing this, couldn't believe he was even contemplating it. But as she relaxed against him, his instincts took over and the tightness in his chest beginning to ease.

He could do this. He loved her and he could take care of her however she needed to be taken care of.

The knowledge came to him suddenly, but he didn't back away from it the way he always thought he would. He loved Rhiannon, loved her with everything inside of him.

After spending years running from himself and his emotions, after trying desperately not to care about anyone after what had happened to Cynthia, Rhiannon had snuck up on his blind side and wrapped herself around his heart when he wasn't looking. But now that she was there—even with all her problems—he wouldn't change a thing.

Taking a deep breath, ignoring his fear and the arousal that appeared despite him, he slid his hands gently into her damp hair, then guided her head back under the spray. When her hair was completely wet, he reached for the shampoo and squeezed a generous amount into his palm before slowly working it into her hair. He stroked her scalp soothingly, his fingers sliding softly through each strand, before he tilted her head back and rinsed the soap away.

He did the same for the conditioner, taking his time, gently rubbing her scalp in a circular motion she seemed to like. Again and again, he massaged her hair until he was sure he had himself under control. Then he rinsed it out, as well.

Though he had just washed her a few minutes before, he grabbed the shower gel again. This time, he squirted it onto his palms and rubbed them together before he began to lather up her body. He started with her neck, moved over the slope of her shoulder down to the small of her back, before sliding around to her stomach and tickling her belly button.

Here the scarring was the worst—he could see the stab wound she had referred to earlier. He traced it with his finger and she shuddered, so he backed away, choosing instead to skim his hands up her rib cage to her breasts.

He cupped the slight weight in his hands, rubbed his thumbs back and forth across her nipples. Rhiannon gasped, arched into him, and her lower body pressed tightly against his erection. Lightning sizzled along his nerve endings and it was his turn to moan.

She grinned, her hands slipping from his waist to palm and squeeze his rear end. "Rhiannon." It was a warning, but she didn't heed it as she trailed her fingers slowly up his spine.

Her scent was driving him insane, wrapping itself around him until all he could smell or feel or taste was her. A combination of his shampoo and her own honeyed sweetness, it touched some possessive chord deep inside him. He loved the idea of her covered in his scent.

Stepping back, he eased her back down onto the

shower bench where he had found her, then sank to his knees between her open thighs.

"What are you doing?" she asked as he slowly lifted her foot and pressed his thumb to her insole.

"I'm loving you, sweetheart. That's all. Just loving you. Relax and enjoy it."

He dug his thumb into the muscles of her foot, making sure not to press too hard, then slipped his hands up her calf. He massaged and kneaded, over and over again until she was all warm and soft, her muscles putty in his hand. He did the same to her other leg, working his way up past her knee to her thighs.

When she was completely relaxed, eyes closed and head lolling against the shower wall, Shawn bent his mouth to her ankle and then licked all the way up the inside of her leg until he reached the hot, welcoming heart of her.

Part of him wanted nothing more than to take her right then, to rip his jeans off and thrust into her until they were both in the throes of ecstasy. But this wasn't about him, and that wasn't what Rhiannon needed.

He eased back, reveling in the soft whimper Rhiannon made as she lost contact with him. Breathing deeply, he struggled to get himself—and his desire—back under control.

When the urgent need to take her subsided, he bent his head back to the long, curvy legs that had been the object of more than a few of his nighttime fantasies. He forced himself to go slow, to savor every inch of her body as his lips caressed her ankle, her calf, the sensitive spot at the back of her knees.

After everything she'd been through, Rhiannon deserved to be loved like this, like she was the most important thing in the world. Because, to him, she was.

He trailed hot kisses along the inside of her thighs, higher and higher until he finally reached her. Taking a deep breath, he pulled her spicy honey scent deep into his lungs. "Rhiannon, baby, is this okay?"

Her eyes opened, dazed, dark chocolate. "What?" she gasped, her body quivering against him.

"Am I hurting you?"

"No. Please. Shawn, please."

He grinned despite himself, then lowered his head, making love to her with his mouth and lips and tongue, thrusting his fingers inside her and stroking her to first one climax and then another.

As the second one hit, she screamed, then melted against him, every bone in her body dissolving until she felt like the warm, sweet honey her scent always reminded him of.

Lifting her in his arms, he turned off the shower with a careless flick of his wrist, then wrapped her in a giant towel and carried her into the bedroom. As he laid her on the bed, her eyes opened sleepily. "What about you?" she murmured, reaching for him.

"Let me take care of you first." He rubbed her dry, spending a long time on her hair, rubbing her scalp and making sure that each strand was as dry as he could get it. By the time he was done, she was sound asleep—exactly as he'd intended.

After drying himself off, he tucked her into bed, then climbed in beside her. But he didn't sleep, he couldn't, as his mind replayed again and again what had happened to Rhiannon in that miserable motel room.

Rage continued to eat at him and as he stared at the ceiling, he wondered if he'd ever be strong enough to move past it.

CHAPTER NINETEEN

RHIANNON AWOKE the next morning, alone and in a strange bed. Jolting upright, she looked around wildly, trying to get her bearings, then calmed down as the events of the previous night came back to her.

She was at Shawn's house, in *his* bed.

She struggled to remember the way things had ended between them. She remembered being in the shower with him and the slow, exquisite way he'd made love to her, remembered him carrying her to the bed and carefully drying her hair. But there was nothing else after that, no culmination of their lovemaking, no cuddling afterward—because she'd fallen asleep! Her cheeks flamed as she realized that, after begging him to make love to her, she had conked out before she could return the favor.

God, was she ever going to make one right step with this man? Seriously, it seemed like every time she tried to do something to get closer to him, it backfired, horribly.

She glanced over to the empty side of the bed. Though the pillow bore the imprint of his head, the sheets were cold. He'd obviously been up for a while. And could she blame him? Why would he want to linger in bed next to a woman who promised him sex not once, but twice—and then failed to deliver both times?

His navy blue robe was draped over a nearby chair, so she shrugged into it—it seemed so much more inviting than the torturous bra-and-panty set she had worn over there last night. Besides, it wasn't like she needed to dress to seduce Shawn. She'd already tried that and failed—miserably.

As she padded through the house, looking for him, she found rooms she hadn't even known existed, despite the fact that she'd hung out at his house numerous times in the past month. She called his name as she cruised past what looked like another living room on the second floor, she was about to give up when she heard someone moving around in a room at the end of the hall. She followed the sound and found Shawn working, his foot tapping to a beat coming from the mp3 player at his ears. No wonder he hadn't heard her call him.

She felt inexplicably shy as she made her way over to him, unsure of how their relationship had changed after the previous night, only knowing that somehow, it had. He looked up as she got closer, and she was shocked at how bad he looked. He had tied his hair back, and his face stood out in stark relief because of it. There were dark circles under his eyes, testament to the fact that he had been up most of the night while she'd slept like a baby, free of nightmares for the first time in longer then she cared to think about.

"How are you feeling?" he asked, pulling the earbuds out of his ears.

"I'm fine." She gave him a tremulous smile. "Better than fine. But did you sleep at all?"

"I caught a few hours—"

"Liar."

He smiled. "Okay, no. I didn't get much sleep."

"I'm sorry about that."

"You need to stop saying that—everything that happens in the world is not your fault."

"Maybe not, but the fact that you couldn't sleep last night certainly was."

"And yet somehow I will survive, bravely forging through my difficult day without sleep."

"You don't have to get sarcastic."

"Actually, with you, sometimes I think I do." He spun his stool around, pulled her into the V between his knees. "So, are you honestly doing okay?"

"I'm doing great. You took really good care of me. Better than I deserve."

His eyes narrowed and she held up a hand. "Okay, I get it. No more self-deprecating comments. I swear."

"We'll see."

She glanced curiously at the board where he was working. "So, tell me about this difficult day of yours. What have you got planned?"

"Oh, I don't know. Maybe a shower, some breakfast. A nap on the couch."

"Wow, that does sound strenuous."

"Exactly. So, do you want to join me?"

"I would love to, but I have an event that starts at one. I have to go home, change clothes and get over there to make sure everything is running smoothly."

"Bummer."

"Yeah."

Silence stretched between them, along with an awkwardness that had never been there before. Rhiannon felt a chill work its way down her spine—was he regretting what had happened between them the night before? Was he wishing he could take it all back?

Not that she would blame him if he did. Yesterday hadn't been a sterling example of her at her most sane.

She cast around for something, anything, to say and settled on work like she always did. "Is this for your deadline?" she asked, nodding at the work he had stretched out on the light board behind them.

"No, that book is pretty much done. This is just me fooling around, trying to get some new ideas."

"It looks cool." She reached out, her finger hovering above the black-and-white drawings. "Can you explain how you do this?"

"Are you sure you want to know? I have a tendency to get carried away when I start talking about my work."

"I'm positive. And feel free to get carried away—I like listening to you talk."

It was all the encouragement he needed. Pulling her closer to the board, he launched into a discussion on storyboarding, explained how he graphed each page out in twelve to sixteen squares before he ever drew a mark.

"I can't believe the amount of work that goes into these things—don't you ever get tired of drawing Shadeslayer?"

"To be honest, no, I don't. Every picture is a little different than the one that came before it." He nodded to a stack of books on a nearby shelf. "You can look at one of those if you want, and see what I'm talking about."

"Oh, I already have them all—I'm about halfway through *Shadeslayer's Doom*. It's good, very interesting. Different than I had expected it to be."

"Different, how?"

"I was shocked at how much work went into it—I mean, it's a full novel with a well-developed story plus the pictures. It must take you a long time to do all that."

"About five months—I used to be faster, but then the books used to be shorter. Now that they're as long as they are, I can only do two a year."

He looked at her curiously. "So, what's a woman like you doing with *Shadeslayer's Doom?* It doesn't exactly seem like your thing."

"Yeah, well, I'm dating this really talented guy who writes all these kick-ass books. He got me hooked on the first three and now it's an addiction. Besides, I figured they might give me some insight into him."

Shawn seemed to hold his breath. "And has it helped you figure him out?"

"I'm not sure yet." She reached a hand out, traced her fingertips over his eyebrows and eyes, across the bridge of his nose and down his jaw to his mouth. He was so incredibly beautiful that it hurt not to touch him, not to love him. "I'll let you know as soon as I get a handle on the last book—and him."

"You do that." He pulled her into his arms, nuzzled her neck. "So, can I make you breakfast? I'm not sure what I've got, but I could probably come up with some eggs and toast."

"No, I'm good. I'll just get my clothes on and get going." She leaned down and brushed her lips across his. "Thank you for last night."

He pulled her in for a longer kiss, and before she knew it, her arms were around his neck, her body plastered to his. "If you thank me or tell me you're sorry one more time, I…"

She watched him curiously. "You'll what?"

"I don't know, but it will be suitably terrible. That much I promise you."

"Ooh, that's big talk. Should I be scared?"

"No. You shouldn't be. Not of me—never of me."

Her stomach clenched. "I didn't mean it that way, Shawn. I was just—"

"I know." He stood. "Come on, I'll walk you back to my bedroom. It's kind of tricky to find it from here."

"Well, if you didn't live in a house the size of a small city, no one would have that problem."

"I told you, it was an investment. I got a good deal on it."

"Right. A good deal. I guess everything's relative."

"I guess so." He grinned at her but it didn't reach his eyes. Rhiannon's stomach rolled sickly as she realized that none of the smiles he'd given her that morning had been normal.

It was starting. She recognized the symptoms—God knew, she had seen them often enough in her family and friends. She had been downgraded from lover to basket case and with that shift came awkwardness, embarrassment and pity.

And this time she had no one to blame but herself.

She picked up the pace—as far as she was concerned, she couldn't get out of there soon enough.

Not that she blamed Shawn for thinking she was crazy—obviously, she'd given him reason. Nor did she blame him for needing some time to assimilate. She'd had three years and still fell to pieces more often than she would like. He certainly had the right to be a little weirded out by everything she had told him the night before, by everything he had seen.

But she didn't want him to be. She knew it was unfair, knew she was asking more from him than she had a right to, but she didn't care. She wanted him for a lover, wanted him for a friend—without all of the bullshit that came along with her past.

Was that really so much to ask?

"So, do you have plans tonight?" she asked as they finally reached his bedroom and she began gathering up her clothes. How could they be in so many places—hadn't she been in bed when Shawn had stripped them off her?

Her cheeks burned as she searched for her underwear and found them under a chair halfway across the room. Obviously, he'd been as eager for her as she'd been for him. Right up until she'd ruined everything.

"Poker night at Robert's. It's our monthly game."

"Cool. Good luck."

"Thanks."

Where was the easy camaraderie, the give-and-take that they were usually so good at? Talking to him was suddenly about as much fun as a trip to the dentist.

She collected her wayward underwear and then took everything into the bathroom, where she dressed as quickly as she could. After washing her face and finger-brushing her teeth—the way Shawn was suddenly acting, she wasn't sure he would appreciate her using his toothbrush—she pulled her hair into a ponytail and then went back into the other room to face him.

She didn't want to, but then she'd spent the past three years doing things she didn't want to do. Why should today be any different?

Shawn was lying on the bed, his back propped against the pillows and his eyes closed. She watched him for a moment, wondering if she would ever have another chance to see him like that. She hoped so, hoped that last night hadn't completely changed his mind about her.

"I'm going now."

His eyelids fluttered but didn't open and she realized that he was more than half asleep. It was strange to see him like that, drowsy, exhausted. He was usually so full of energy and life that it was hard to imagine him ever being this tired. But he was, his exhaustion written clearly in the unfamiliar lines on his face.

Tiptoeing over to the bed, Rhiannon pulled the covers over him, then—because she couldn't resist—bent down and kissed him softly on the cheek.

His eyes snapped open. "Hey."

"I'm sorry. I didn't mean to wake you. Go back to sleep—I'll let myself out."

"No, stay." His fingers circled her wrist and tugged until she was sitting on the bed next to him. Then he wrapped an arm over her thighs, put his head in her lap and promptly went back to sleep.

She sat there for a while, stroking his hair, watching him sleep. Enjoying the feel of his body, warm against her own, along with the absence of fear.

The clock on his nightstand clicked away the minutes and she knew she should leave—if she stayed much longer she was going to be late getting to the hotel to set-up for the Markinson wedding. But she couldn't bring herself to move, not when holding Shawn—and being held by him— brought her more peace than anything had in a very long time.

Things would be okay, she told herself. Once Shawn got over his shock, they could talk. They could clear the air and then get back to normal. Maybe, if she was lucky, she could even talk him into trying to make love to her again—with the lights on this time, since he'd already seen every scar she had in the shower the night before.

He was warm and strong and comfortable and she felt herself getting drowsy. She fought it off—she couldn't afford to fall asleep. Plus, she didn't want to miss any of this time with Shawn.

Eventually, though, she couldn't put off the inevitable. She gingerly moved Shawn's arm from where it rested on her thigh, then did her best to slip out from under him without waking him up.

As she lowered his head to the pillow, he frowned. "Cynthia, no. Don't go."

At first, she wasn't sure she'd heard him correctly. But when he rolled over and mumbled the name again, she knew she had.

Her heart plummeted to the floor.

The entire time she'd been holding him, weaving dreams of what it would be like to have a real relationship with Shawn, what it would feel like to make love to him and hold him and be held by him, he'd been dreaming of another woman.

She started backing away, wanting nothing more than to escape, but by the time she'd made it to the door his eyes were open and he was wide-awake.

"I'm sorry. I didn't mean to wake you up. Go back

to sleep. I'll just let myself out. The door locks automatically and—" She was babbling like an idiot. Snapping her mouth shut, she ducked through the bedroom door and all but ran down the hallway toward the front door.

"Rhiannon, wait!" Shawn's voice was husky with sleep but it didn't slow him down any. Within seconds, he was barreling down the hallway after her.

"What's wrong?"

"Who's Cynthia?" She clapped a hand over her mouth, furious with herself for asking. The man had been sleeping, for God's sake. She had no business being upset over what happened in his dreams.

She started to apologize, to tell him it was none of her business, but he seemed to shut down right in front of her. His eyes went from warm and confused to icy and reserved as his jaw tightened and his hands clenched into fists at his sides.

"Where did you hear that name?"

"You said it while you were asleep. I'm sorry, I shouldn't pry. It's none of my business—"

"You're my girlfriend," he answered, as if that said it all. And maybe it did—she couldn't deny that hearing him say it sent a little thrill through her.

He rubbed a hand over his face, cursed thoroughly. "Cynthia was my fiancée, way back when."

He'd been engaged? The news sent Rhiannon reeling, had her adjusting everything she'd ever thought about Shawn and his commitment issues. But why hadn't he told her he'd been engaged—why had he kept it a secret? She couldn't call him on it—after all, she'd kept a much bigger secret—but still, it made her wonder.

"Oh. Okay." She knew she should leave, should head out the door without asking any more questions. He was certainly entitled to his privacy. She even started to go, but in the end, she couldn't walk out the door she'd opened. Not before asking, "So, why did you break up?"

She actually saw him brace himself, as if expecting a powerful blow. It scared her more than anything else had, the fact that he obviously still had powerful feelings regarding Cynthia. "We didn't."

"I'm sorry?"

"She killed herself, three months before our wedding. She was clinically depressed and nothing I did could reach her. I came home one afternoon and found her. I'm sorry. I don't know why I dreamed about her now—it's been a long time since I've had one of those nightmares."

Horror shot through her as his words sunk in. Wedding. Killed herself. Found her. Nightmares. Shawn's happy-go-lucky facade had been hiding a past almost as dark as her own. He'd moved on, obviously, better than she had, but still, he had suffered. And her breakdown last night had brought it all back.

She thought back to the way he'd looked this morning when she'd found him, drawn and pale and miserable. She had done that to him. She had brought all the pain of his past back to him, in spades.

"Oh, no. Oh, I'm so sorry, Shawn. I never meant—"

"Never meant what?" He looked confused. "Rhiannon, this isn't your fault."

"I have to go."

"What? Now? Don't you want to talk?"

"I can't. I—" Her head was spinning with the amount of destruction she'd caused, with the amount of pain she'd brought down on Shawn because she was too weak to handle her own past.

"I'm sorry." She reached a hand up, caressed his cheek. "So very sorry."

And then she ran, desperate to get to her car—and out of Shawn's sight—before she broke down yet again.

CHAPTER TWENTY

SHAWN STARED AFTER RHIANNON, too shocked by the events of the past few minutes to even chase after her. Stalking into the kitchen, he grabbed his phone and dialed her cell number. It rang a few times before voicemail picked up and he bit back a curse. "This is Shawn," he said after the beep. "Call me. We need to talk."

What the hell had spooked her so badly? Sure he could have told her about Cynthia with a little more finesse, but what did she want from him? She'd blindsided him with the name when he'd still been half-asleep and the story had just kind of poured out of him.

Was that any reason for her to take off like that, without even telling him what had her so upset?

Furious with himself for falling asleep before he and Rhiannon could talk, furious with her because she'd used Cynthia as an excuse to run away, he reached for the phone and dialed again. She still didn't answer and he left another message. And another one and another one.

All through the day he kept calling, waiting for her to pick up. How long did a damn wedding take, anyway? he wondered as he drove to Robert's around eight that evening. Surely she'd gotten one of the million messages he'd left for her by then, but still she hadn't bothered to pick up.

By the time he'd gotten to his friend's house, he'd moved from frustrated to annoyed to downright angry with her. Was this what he was supposed to expect from now on—that whenever she got upset with him she just froze him out? Ignored him like he was some pesky fly who wasn't worth her time?

Like hell. If she thought this was how she was going to act every time they fought, then she was in for a rude awakening. Because he was done putting up with her crap.

He knocked on Robert's door harder than he needed to, then waited impatiently for his friend to answer. The sooner they got started, the sooner Poker Night would be over and he could head over to Rhiannon's and demand to know what was going on in that mixed-up head of hers. Because obviously something was, and he'd missed out on it.

"Whoa, dude, who pissed in your cornflakes?" Robert asked as soon as he opened the door. "You look like you could chew through a metal rod and then start on a skyscraper."

He slammed the six-pack of beer he'd bought into Robert's hands. "Nothing. Are the other guys here?"

"Yeah. We've been waiting for you."

"Sorry. Let's get started." He shrugged out of his jacket and headed to Robert's game room, where they always played.

"All right, then." Robert followed him up the stairs. "I'm fine, thanks for asking. I guess I don't have to ask how you're doing?"

Shawn shot him a look that had his friend shutting

up posthaste. When he made it to the top of the stairs, it was to find the other three guys they played cards with—Jackson, Luc and David—lounging around on the sofa and cracking jokes.

"You ready to play?" he grunted.

All three looked up in surprise. "Yeah, sure," Jackson stood up, extended his hand. "How've you been?"

Shawn shook his hand. "Fine."

The other men exchanged a look and Robert said, "Woman problems."

"Obviously. What's the matter? You juggling too many again, Shawn?" Luc parked himself at the table with a laugh.

"Are we going to play or what?" Shawn responded.

"Absolutely." David grabbed the cards and started to shuffle. "What's the minimum bid?"

"Twenty," answered Robert as he settled himself at the table next to Shawn, plopping a beer in front of each of them.

"Right."

As his friends laughed and joked around him, Shawn glowered and drank his beer. He felt like a total asshole, but he was still too mad at Rhiannon to concentrate on anything else. Of course, the guys didn't seem to mind because by the time the fourth hand rolled around, he'd already dropped two hundred bucks.

They were a couple of hands from the end when David said, "You know, much as I like taking your money, Shawn, I'm starting to feel a little guilty. You want to tell us what's got your panties in such a wad, or are we supposed to guess?"

He folded, pushed back from the table. "Look, I'm sorry, man. I need to go. My girlfriend—" He stopped because he didn't know how to go about explaining how complicated his and Rhiannon's simple relationship had suddenly become. "I should probably go straighten things out with her and spare you my attitude problems."

When none of them said anything, when even Luc refrained from messing with him, Shawn figured he must look as wrecked as he felt. He let himself out the front door and drove over to Rhiannon's place. He called her one more time from the road and when she still didn't answer, his anger shot back up to the stratosphere and stayed there until she opened her apartment door.

"I've been calling you all day," he said with no preamble. "You couldn't pick up the phone and talk to me?"

"I was working."

He eyed her pajamas. "Really? You're working now?"

"You said you were going to a poker game tonight— I didn't want to be one of those women who called a guy when he was with his friends."

"I left early."

"I can see that." She stepped back, opened the door wider. "Do you want to come in?"

He didn't bother to answer her, just stormed into the condo. "You want to tell me what's going on, Rhiannon?"

"I've been busy all day—"

"So busy you couldn't answer a phone call? You've never been that busy before."

"You don't need to get sarcastic with me."

"Then tell me what the hell is happening here! I

thought after last night that we were getting somewhere, you know? But now you've shut me out more
completely than ever and I want to know why." He
closed the distance between them. "I'm sorry I said
Cynthia's name today. It didn't mean anything—"

"I'm not upset about that."

"You're not?" He eyed her carefully, tried to figure
out what was going on in her brain. "Then, what? Because you're not going to convince me something didn't
set you off."

"It's nothing. Really," she continued as he started to
protest. "I just got overwhelmed with everything that
happened, you know? It was a crazy night and I needed
some space."

He did know—he'd spent half the day going over
everything that she'd told him and trying to figure out
where they were supposed to go from there. He loved
her, wanted her, but she was still holding herself away
from him. Afraid to trust, afraid to love. He understood,
but understanding didn't make it any easier for him to
accept.

"I'm sorry I fell asleep this morning—we never
really got a chance to talk."

She shrugged, but the smile she sent him was real—
even if it was smaller than he was used to. "I'm sorry
I fell asleep last night. Believe me, that wasn't how I'd
planned on the evening ending."

"Rhiannon, it's no big deal. I can wait."

She nodded, looked away. "You want something to
drink? I think I've got a half-open bottle of wine in the
fridge, if you'd like a glass."

"I don't want wine." He wrapped an arm around her

waist—slowly, carefully—and pulled her toward him
before settling on the sofa, Rhiannon in his lap.

"I just want to hold you for a while. Is that okay?"

"Yeah." She cleared her throat. "It's more than
okay."

"Good." He tucked her head under his chin and
settled back on the sofa to watch whatever chick flick
she had on the TV. And wonder how he was going to
get into Rhiannon's head long enough to figure what
was really going on in there.

SHAWN WAS ASLEEP. Not dozing like he'd been at his
house that morning, but really truly asleep. Rhiannon
slowly disentangled herself from him making sure
not to wake him this time—and then went into her
bedroom to retrieve a blanket for him.

As she was covering him, she couldn't help looking at Shawn—really looking at him, for the first time
since he'd shown up at her apartment. If possible, he
looked worse than he had earlier that morning.

His skin was sallow, his eyes sunken, and the dark
circles from earlier had somehow gotten deeper. As she
looked at him, she remembered what he'd said weeks
before, about serious not being a good look for him.
He'd been right. He looked like he'd aged ten years in
the past twenty-four hours.

She'd messed with his head and his body and his
emotions, had gotten them both so turned around that
neither of them knew which way was up. She hated
herself for dragging this strong, beautiful, kindhearted
man into the mayhem with her.

She just wished she knew how she could fix it. That's
what she'd been thinking about all day, as she'd dodged

phone call after phone call. How to get herself—and him—out of the mess their relationship had become.

Because he didn't deserve this, didn't deserve getting stuck with her after he'd already lived with the suicidal Cynthia. How much could one man be expected to take, after all?

Oh, she knew Shawn, knew he would never complain about the truckload of baggage she brought with her. Just like she knew he was too decent to break up with her now, when she was at her most vulnerable. But he had to be feeling trapped—how else could he be feeling after finding himself with another screwed-up girlfriend?

He'd seemed shocked that he had dreamed of Cynthia that morning, but she wasn't. One night with her and her myriad neuroses and he was right back there, in the middle of the nightmare he'd lived with Cynthia.

No, Shawn wouldn't walk out on her now any more than he had walked out on his fiancée. But that didn't mean it was right for her to let him stay. They'd both been clear when they had started this whole thing— they were both looking for a bit of fun, something casual. Something relaxed.

Well, after last night there was nothing casual or relaxed about their relationship, and that wasn't fair to Shawn. She'd sprung her nightmare on him, wrapped him up in it and hadn't so much as asked him if he wanted to be there. She'd changed the rules and he was too nice of a guy to change them back.

So she'd have to do it for him.

She sat there watching him for most of the night, trying to figure out the best way to break things off. By the time the sun finally came over the horizon, lighting up her apartment with the roses and lavenders of early morning, she knew exactly what she was going to do.

So, after taking a quick shower and getting dressed for work, she wrote Shawn a casual, friendly note. *Shawn, I've got an early start today so I snuck out while you were sleeping. Feel free to stay as long as you like, and lock up on your way out—there's an extra key above the fridge. I'll be in touch soon about the party.* Then left the apartment without a backward glance.

She spent the morning at work thinking about how she wasn't going to think about Shawn, and when Logan stuck his head in her office to tell her that Shawn was on the phone, she was almost relieved. At least now she could put her plan into action.

"Tell him I'm tied up with a client and that I'll call him back."

Logan's brow rose quizzically. "But you aren't tied up with a client."

"I'm about to be." She picked up the phone and started to dial.

"Rhiannon." She paused as Logan's voice cut through the ice she had wrapped around herself that morning.

"What?"

"Are you sure you know what you're doing?"

"Of course, why?"

"It's just— Shawn's a great guy."

He was, absolutely, which was why she was going to end it with him as coldly and bloodlessly as possible. He deserved better than what she could give him.

CHAPTER TWENTY-ONE

SHAWN WALKED AROUND his backyard, staring at all the carnival games set up and wondering if today was going to be the day he finally saw Rhiannon. It had been eleven days since she'd left him sleeping on the sofa in her apartment, six days since he'd seen or spoken to her.

He'd done everything he could to talk to her—had staked out her condo, had shown up at her workplace, had called and emailed and sent flowers. All to no avail. She'd cut him completely out of her life and without so much as an explanation.

Oh, he supposed the voicemail she'd left him on the third day counted, in her mind, as an explanation, but it sure as hell didn't count that way for him. *I'm sorry. I'm not ready to do this after all.* But ten words didn't exactly provide the means for a dialogue.

That was Rhiannon for you. Once she made up her mind, there was no changing it—or at least, that's what Logan had told him when he'd tried again and again to get into her office to see her.

He didn't believe that, couldn't believe it. He loved her too much to just give up on them because Rhiannon was scared. He'd find a way to fix things between them. He had to, because spending the rest of his life without her didn't bear thinking about.

He'd been waiting for this morning for what seemed like forever, had planned on cornering Rhiannon when she got here to oversee the set-up and make her talk to him. She must have known, because she'd sent Logan instead. Her boss had promised him that Rhiannon was going to be at the party later that afternoon, but the look on his face told Shawn all he needed—and didn't want—to know.

Rhiannon had closed herself off completely and Logan didn't think there was a chance in hell that Shawn could reach her.

He glanced at his watch. It was one-thirty—two hours before the first guests were set to arrive and fifteen minutes after Rhiannon was supposed to be there. There was still no sign of her. Not that he was surprised. It would be just like her to try to sweep in five minutes before the guests were due and then claim to be too busy to talk.

Well, he wasn't putting up with it any longer. He felt like he'd done nothing these past few weeks besides wait for Rhiannon. He'd waited for her to see him. Waited for her to want him. And now he was waiting again—for a chance to convince her to give them one more try.

Too bad he didn't have a clue how to go about doing that.

He picked up a beanbag, threw it as hard as he could into the giant shark's mouth in front of him. It hit with a satisfying thump and before he knew it, he'd picked up all of the remaining beanbags and was firing them at the shark, one right after the other. Some made it in the mouth, some hit outside, but it didn't matter. It was the act of throwing something—of doing something besides impotently waiting—that he'd been looking for.

"Shawn."

At first, he thought he had imagined Rhiannon's voice, but when he turned toward it, there she was, dressed in a long-sleeved, scarlet blouse and a pair of skintight jeans that showed off her incredible legs. Her hair was up today, but the wind had coaxed a few strands into tumbling down around her face and shoulders. She looked beautiful and sexy and so good that he could barely believe she was real.

"The caterers are setting up in your kitchen," she said. "I hope you don't mind that I let them in."

He had a speech planned, one he'd worked on for days as he'd tried to figure out a way to get her to listen to him. He opened his mouth, prepared to start with it, but what came out instead was, "That's *it?* After eleven days of pretending I don't exist, all you have to say to me is that the caterers are in my kitchen? Have you lost your mind?"

"Can we talk about this later? I've got party details—"

"Screw the party." He stormed across the lawn at her, grabbed her elbow in a none-too-gentle grip and all but dragged her into the house and down the hall to his bedroom.

"I guess there's no chance we can be reasonable about his, hmm?" She looked at him like he was a child in the middle of a temper tantrum. Her cool only ratcheted his anger up a notch.

"If I hadn't been reasonable, I would have stormed into your office and dragged you out by the hair days ago."

"Logan—"

"Screw Logan."

"That seems to be your answer to everything today."

"Damn it, Rhiannon. Why would you do that to me? To us?"

"It's for the best. Things were getting out of hand and I thought a clean break would make them easier."

"Out of hand? I love you and you just cut me off at the knees like I was nothing. Like the way I feel about you is nothing."

"That's not true. You don't—"

"Don't tell me how I feel. You seem to think that you can control everything here, that you get to make all the choices for both of us. But that's not how this is going to work. We're in a relationship whether you like it or not, and I am not going to be frozen out because you're too scared to try to make it work."

"That's not what happened." The words burst from her and he watched, fascinated, as her mask cracked right down the middle. Her face crumpled and she turned away.

He followed her, unwilling to let her get her composure back. "Well, if that's not how it was, tell me, please. How was it?"

When she turned to him this time, it was the Rhiannon he knew and loved staring back at him. "I'm bad for you."

He waited for her to say more, and when she didn't, he asked, "What the hell is that supposed to mean?"

"You didn't see yourself after that night—you looked terrible. Exhausted, strung out, in pain. I couldn't stand it."

"The woman I loved had just told me that she had

been brutally raped. How the hell was I supposed to look—I was devastated."

"I dragged you into my problems, wrapped you up in them when we had promised to keep things casual. How could I ask you to stay with me when all I kept doing was hurting you?"

"I'm a big boy, Rhiannon. I could have left anytime I wanted."

"But you wouldn't. You're too nice for your own good."

He barked out a laugh. "Don't count on that, baby. I've spent years dodging around women and their issues, refusing to be drawn in beyond the most casual connection. I'll be the first to admit Cynthia did a number on me and I'm not proud of how I handled my subsequent relationships with women, but I'm not going to sugarcoat it, either. I never stuck around for the rough stuff."

"Bull. You think I don't know you? You think I don't know what a decent person you are? You never once tried to duck out on me, no matter how freaked out I was."

"You're not listening to me, Rhiannon. I stayed because I couldn't leave. I took one look at your crazy hair and that dimple of yours and I fell. Hard. I love you and your neuroses. You can push me as hard as you want and it won't matter. I'm not going anywhere."

"I don't want to be another Cynthia. I don't want you having nightmares about me years from now because you couldn't help me. Because I couldn't be helped."

"Cynthia was a manic-depressive who wouldn't stay on her medication and rejected everything the doctors and I did to help her. You are *nothing* like Cynthia."

"You don't know what you're talking about—"

"No, you're the one who doesn't know what she's talking about. I loved Cynthia and I watched her self-destruct."

"And now you say you love me and I'm about to do the very same thing."

"Honey, you're so far from self-destruction that you wouldn't recognize it if it smacked you in the face. You're strong and you're such a fighter. You're on the brink of reclaiming everything—your life, your sexuality, your heart. Don't sell yourself short because you're afraid of hurting me."

"But you can't love me!" she wailed.

"Why not?"

"Because I'm a mess. You saw what I did to you that last night—"

"What did you do to me, besides share the most personal, private side of you? What did you do except let me love you?"

"But I didn't."

"You did." He reached for her, pulled her into his arms. This time she didn't fight him. "And you may be a mess, but you're my mess. And I'm not letting you go. No matter how hard you push, I'm just going to push back until you're willing to accept how I feel about you."

She buried her face in the curve of his neck. "God, Shawn, I love you so much. I don't want to hurt you anymore."

"What did you say?" This time he was the one who pulled away so that he could get a good look at her face.

"I don't want to hurt you—"

"Not that. The other."

There were tears rolling down her face, but she was smiling. "Oh, you mean the part about me loving you."

"Say it," he growled. "Look me in the eye and say it to me again."

"I love you, Shawn. I think I've always loved you. But I'm scared."

"Don't be scared, baby. I'm right here."

"But that's what I'm scared of. I don't want to hurt you."

"Rhiannon, sweetheart, the only thing you've done to hurt me is to cut me out of your life. As for the rest, I feel privileged to be along for the ride."

It was her turn to study him, her turn to look deep into his eyes and see the truth. When she did, she wrapped her arms around his neck and pulled his lips down to hers.

He kissed her, savoring the feel of her against him. Reveling in the fact that she was once again back where she belonged. When he could take the sensual tension between them no longer, however, he pulled away and slowly stripped off his T-shirt.

"Shawn?" She reached for him, the look in her eyes so sweetly uncertain that a part of him wanted to tell her they could wait forever. That he didn't need the physical side of their relationship until she was ready for it.

But he'd learned from the last time, knew now just how important it was for her to know that he was satisfied with her. Until he made love to her she would never feel secure, never feel like she could give him what he needed.

She was crazy, her thinking completely wrong, but he knew her well enough to know that on this, there would be no changing her mind.

But instead of explaining, he simply said, "Trust me, Rhiannon," then brushed his lips over her forehead, her eyes. He slid them down the sharp angles of her cheeks to the smooth line of her jaw. Nibbled at that strong, delicious jaw for a while, delighting in the small, broken breaths that eased from her.

When he'd exhausted the possibilities on her glorious, giving face, he slipped lower. Using his lips and tongue softly—so softly—he traced the elegant curve of her neck. Skimmed slowly over the hollows of her collarbone. Nuzzled his way between breasts. Nudged her blouse up and over her head. Divested her of her bra. Then delivered one long, slow lick from her navel to her breastbone.

Rhiannon gasped, arched, while her hands moved restlessly over his shoulders and back. "Shh," he whispered, unbuttoning her jeans and easing them down her legs.

She was wearing panties as soft and pink as she was. Cut high in the hips, they rode low over her flat belly and he grinned as he slipped his tongue under the waistband.

She jerked, trembled, clutching at his hair to hold him in place.

But he would have none of it. He drew back so that he could look up at her. "You're in control here, Rhiannon. You tell me what you want and how much. And no matter what's happening, if you want me to stop, you tell me and I'll stop."

"I know it's you, Shawn, and I know you won't hurt me. Make love to me. Please."

Moving out from beneath her grasping hands, he stood and stripped off his clothes in a few quick movements. Then he was sinking onto the bed with her, pulling her into the circle of his arms. Relishing the feel of this woman he loved more than he'd ever loved anyone pressed so tightly against him.

Rhiannon wrapped her arms around Shawn, holding him as tightly against her as she could manage. It felt so right to be here with him, to cradle his head against her breast as her body yearned for his. She prayed with everything inside of her that she wouldn't mess it up, that she wouldn't end up turning him away again.

"Shawn, I'm sor—"

He cut her words off with a kiss, so tender, so exquisite that it brought a new tightness to the lump at the back of her throat. "Don't," he whispered, his wicked blue eyes calmer than she'd ever seen them.

Leaning her head to the side, eyes still locked with his, she offered him her mouth again. He took it and the sudden pressure of his lips on hers was like finding herself again—sweet, warm and so familiar that it brought tears to her eyes.

A groan rumbled low in his chest and she grinned— thrilled at how easily she could make this strong, powerful man want her. Equally excited about how quickly he could do the same to her.

His hands weren't steady as they shimmied her panties down her legs, but they were capable. Everywhere they touched ignited a small fire within her, every skim of his fingers was a little zing adding to the emotions already pulsing within her.

"You're beautiful," he murmured as he caressed her ankle with tender lips, his lips running along her scars with a tenderness and appreciation that couldn't be faked.

She wanted to be. For him, she wanted to be everything. Sliding her hands down his spine, she toyed with the rigid muscles under her hands. So strong, so capable, so ready to take on her problems as his own. What had she ever done to deserve him?

She started to tell him how she felt, but he silenced the words with another kiss. And then he was rolling across the bed, spinning with her, lifting her above him as his mouth swept over the curve of her breast.

He settled her astride him gently, her knees on either side of his hips. "You're in control, Rhiannon. You take as much or as little of me as you want."

She paused, savoring the feel of him against her. And then—with a single fluid motion—made them one.

She rode him slowly, sweetly, cherishing him with her body the way he so obviously cherished her. Immersed in him, wrapped up in the feelings that arced between them with each slow glide of her body, she kept the rhythm languid, steady.

Even as the tension began to build in her, the ache between her thighs becoming more and more unbearable, she kept it dreamy, drowsy.

Even as his hips arched beneath hers, and the hands that had caressed her so gently turned rough in an instant, she kept it leisurely, lazy.

Need was a living thing within her, but she pushed it back again and again, unwilling to have their moment end so soon. She'd waited so long for this, to be held in the arms of a lover who understood and treasured her, that she wanted it to last forever.

But the need continued to build until sweat poured from him, from her, mingled as she leaned over him and brushed a kiss across the muscles directly over his heart.

"Now, Rhiannon!" Shawn's hands clamped on her thighs like a vise. "Please, I need you. I need you now."

There they were, the words she'd been waiting to hear all along, without even knowing it. Because she was suddenly as desperate as he was, she let him take control for the last few seconds. One powerful thrust, another, and they plunged over the edge of the world. Together.

When it was over, when she was wrapped in Shawn's arms and her heart had finally slowed to something resembling normal, she told him in the clearest voice she could muster, "I love you."

"Good. Because you're going to marry me."

"Really?" She lifted her head and stared at him. "It's customary for a man to ask a woman if she wants to marry him."

"Yeah, well, it's customary for the woman not to drive the man who loves her completely around the bend, and that hasn't stopped you."

"Funny." But she settled on the bed next to him, her head cushioned by his rock solid biceps. "We both know I'm too old for you."

"Shouldn't I be the one to decide that?" he asked. "Or maybe what you really mean is that I'm too young for you?"

"Yeah, right." But when she looked into his warm,

summer-sky eyes she couldn't help smiling. Shawn would take care of her, in sickness and in health. In good times and in bad—and she would do the same for him. He was that kind of man.

Still, there was no reason to make it too easy for him. "We both know I only keep you around because I like the idea of my own personal boy toy."

"Do you, now?"

"I do." She reached between them, stroked him, reveling in the way his breath caught and his eyes turned smoky. "Unless you object?"

"Well, if you insist." He sighed heavily. "It's a burden I'm prepared to bear if it means keeping you happy."

"Oh, I insist, all right." She rolled on top of him, took him inside her again.

"Thank God."

He arched beneath her and she gasped as pleasure shot through every nerve ending she had. She started to lower her head to kiss him, but he stopped her with a finger on her lips. "Marry me, Rhiannon. I don't want to live without you."

"Just try to stop me."

And then he was kissing her and she was kissing him right back, giving herself up to the joy and love she had found where she had least expected it.

* * * * *

HARLEQUIN SuperRomance®

COMING NEXT MONTH

Available January 11, 2011

REQUEST YOUR FREE BOOKS!

2 FREE NOVELS PLUS 2 FREE GIFTS!

HARLEQUIN®

Super Romance®

Exciting, emotional, unexpected!

YES! Please send me 2 FREE Harlequin® Superromance® novels and my 2 FREE gifts (gifts are worth about $10). After receiving them, if I don't wish to receive any more books, I can return the shipping statement marked "cancel." If I don't cancel, I will receive 6 brand-new novels every month and be billed just $4.69 per book in the U.S. or $5.24 per book in Canada. That's a saving of at least 15% off the cover price! It's quite a bargain! Shipping and handling is just 50¢ per book.* I understand that accepting the 2 free books and gifts places me under no obligation to buy anything. I can always return a shipment and cancel at any time. Even if I never buy another book from Harlequin, the two free books and gifts are mine to keep forever.

135/336 HDN E5P4

Name _____ (PLEASE PRINT)

Address _____ Apt. #

City _____ State/Prov. _____ Zip/Postal Code

Signature (if under 18, a parent or guardian must sign)

Mail to the **Harlequin Reader Service:**
IN U.S.A.: P.O. Box 1867, Buffalo, NY 14240-1867
IN CANADA: P.O. Box 609, Fort Erie, Ontario L2A 5X3

Not valid for current subscribers to Harlequin Superromance books.

**Are you a current subscriber to Harlequin Superromance books
and want to receive the larger-print edition?
Call 1-800-873-8635 today!**

* Terms and prices subject to change without notice. Prices do not include applicable taxes. N.Y. residents add applicable sales tax. Canadian residents will be charged applicable provincial taxes and GST. Offer not valid in Quebec. This offer is limited to one order per household. All orders subject to approval. Credit or debit balances in a customer's account(s) may be offset by any other outstanding balance owed by or to the customer. Please allow 4 to 6 weeks for delivery. Offer available while quantities last.

Your Privacy: Harlequin Books is committed to protecting your privacy. Our Privacy Policy is available online at www.eHarlequin.com or upon request from the Reader Service. From time to time we make our lists of customers available to reputable third parties who may have a product or service of interest to you. If you would prefer we not share your name and address, please check here. ☐

Help us get it right—We strive for accurate, respectful and relevant communications. To clarify or modify your communication preferences, visit us at www.ReaderService.com/consumerchoice.

HSR10R

HARLEQUIN®

A Romance

FOR EVERY MOOD™

Spotlight on

Classic

Quintessential, modern love stories
that are romance at its finest.

See the next page
to enjoy a sneak peek from
the Harlequin Presents® series.

*Harlequin Presents® is thrilled
to introduce the first installment of
an epic tale of passion and drama by*
**USA TODAY Bestselling Author
Penny Jordan!**

*When buttoned-up Giselle first meets
the devastatingly handsome Saul Parenti,
the heat between them is explosive....*

"LET ME GET THIS STRAIGHT. Are you actually suggesting
that I would stoop to that kind of game playing?"

Saul came out from behind his desk and walked toward
her. Giselle could smell his hot male scent and it was making
her dizzy, igniting a low, dull, pulsing ache that was taking
over her whole body.

Giselle defended her suspicions. "You don't want me here."

"No," Saul agreed, "I don't."

And then he did what he had sworn he would not do,
cursing himself beneath his breath as he reached for her,
pulling her fiercely into his arms and kissing her with all
the pent-up fury she had aroused in him from the moment
he had first seen her.

Giselle certainly *wanted* to resist him. But the hand she
raised to push him away developed a will of its own and
was sliding along his bare arm beneath the sleeve of his
shirt, and the body that should have been arching away
from him was instead melting into him.

Beneath the pressure of his kiss he could feel and taste
her gasp of undeniable response to him. He wanted to
devour her, take her and drive them both until they were
equally satiated—even whilst the anger within him that
she should make him feel that way roared and burned its

HPEXP0111

resentment of his niced.

She was helpless, Giselle recognized, totally unable to withstand the storm lashing at her, able only to cling to the man who was the cause of it and pray that she would survive.

Somewhere else in the building a door banged. The sound exploded into the sensual tension that had enclosed them, driving them apart. Saul's chest was rising and falling as he fought for control; Giselle's whole body was trembling.

Without a word she turned and ran.

Find out what happens when Saul and Giselle succumb to their irresistible desire in

THE RELUCTANT SURRENDER

Available January 2011 from Harlequin Presents®

©2010 Penny Jordan

HPEXP0111

Silhouette *Desire*

HAVE BABY,
NEED BILLIONAIRE

MAUREEN CHILD

Simon Bradley is accomplished, successful and very proud. The fact that he has to prove he's fit to be a father to his own child is preposterous. Especially when he has to prove it to Tula Barrons, one of the most scatterbrained women he's ever met. But Simon has a ruthless plan to win Tula over and when passion overrules prudence one night, it opens up the door to an affair that leaves them both staggering. Will this billionaire bachelor learn to love more than his fortune?

Billionaires and Babies

*Available January
wherever books are sold.*

Always Powerful, Passionate and Provocative.

Visit Silhouette Books at www.eHarlequin.com

SD73072

MARGARET WAY

Wealthy Australian, Secret Son

Rohan was Charlotte's shining white knight
until he disappeared—before she had
the chance to tell him she was pregnant.

But when Rohan returns years later as
a self-made millionaire, could the blond,
blue-eyed little boy and Charlotte's heart
keep him from leaving again?

Available January 2011

www.eHarlequin.com

HRI7704